THREE LAMPS
and
Other Polish Tales

translated

by Sergiej Nowikow

The book comprises 50 folk tales.
The tales were translated in 2016
and had never been published
in English before.
Be sure to choose the compilation
for the best fairy tales ever written.
Children's fairy tales teach our
little ones to be both civil and
creative while helping them develop
important personal traits.

Copyright © 2013 Sergiy Novikov
All rights reserved.
No part of this publication may be reproduced, distributed, or transmitted in any
form or by any means, including photocopying, recording, or other electronic
or mechanical methods, without the prior written permission of the publisher,
except in the case of brief quotations embodied in critical reviews.

Printed in the United States of America

ISBN-13: 978-1517127992
ISBN-10: 1517127998

Other books from this series can be found at the following locations:

**The Comédienne,
For the Love of Children**
by Wladyslaw S. Reymont
www.amazon.com/dp/1530484367
The Comédienne. This is the story of a girl who comes to the capital to make a theater career. She meets corrupt, jealous, hysterical, and vulgar people lacking high principles and interests.
For the Love of Children is a curiously plotted work by Wladyslaw S.Reymont. The main storyline deals with the relations between a poor boy and a girl from a rich family. This is the translation by S.Nowikow. It also includes awesome illustrations that go right along with the story. This is the first publication of the translation. Wladyslaw S. Reymont is the **1924** laureate of the Nobel Prize in Literature.

**In Desert and Wilderness,
The Story of a Lighthouse Keeper**
by Henryk Sienkiewicz
www.amazon.com/dp/1530494303
In Desert and Wilderness.
The book describes the wanderings of two children in Africa. It is a fascinating narrative full of adventure.
The Story of a Lighthouse Keeper.
It is an overwhelming story of a retired elderly soldier who takes the job of a lighthouse keeper in the Caribbean Sea. This is the translation by S.Nowikow, which is easy to read and understand. It is one of the best translations of the work ever published. The book includes more than 100 illustrations. Henryk Sienkiewicz is the **1905** laureate of the Nobel Prize in Literature.

These fairy tales share
with you the wisdom and experience
of many generations of Polish people.

If you want to feel the humor
of this wonderful nation
and get a glimpse of the people's kindness,
you are welcome to read these wonderful tales.

SERMON

A monk was caught by robbers when crossing a border. They surrounded him. Their chief told the monk, "Give us a sermon to our taste, or else we will kill you."

The poor monk began to tremble, thinking, "Sure they will if I fail."

He prayed to Saint Bartholomew, the patron saint of those skinned alive, using a tree stub as an ambon. The robbers took their hats off and listened to him.

The monk crossed himself and began, "Your life is extremely similar to the life of our Lord Jesus Christ."

"Why on earth?" the robbers asked, bursting with joy.

"I will tell you why," the monk said. "Our Lord Jesus was born to a poor family. So were you. As a child, our Lord Jesus would help Saint Joseph timber. You did not laze about either; otherwise your dads would have beaten the living daylights out of you. When our Lord Jesus had grown older, he went on a pilgrimage. So do you wander around. Lord Jesus was caught; and so will you. Lord Jesus was whipped; and so will you. Lord Jesus was crucified; so will each of you be hanged. Jesus descended to hell; so will you. That is it. Did you enjoy my sermon?"

"Of course we did," the robbers said. "We enjoyed it greatly!"

Their chief was generous enough to give some gold coins to the monk. Having walked a safe distance away, the monk turned back to the robbers shouting, "I did not finish though! Lord Jesus ascended to Heaven, which you will not do!"

THREE LAMPS

A boy once went to the woods to pick mushrooms. He got to the thickest of the forest and suddenly heard somebody shouting, crying, and begging for help. The boy ran to where the sound was coming from. He saw a deep, bottomless swamp, and an old woman bogged down and thrashing about helplessly.

The boy threw some brushwood onto a hillock hurriedly, got himself a stick, came up to the old woman, and held the stick out for her. The old woman grabbed the stick so hard that she nearly drew the boy into the bog.

The lad had just turned fifteen; his strength had not fully developed yet; but he was not too weak. Somehow he managed to pull the old woman out.

When he could see whom he had rescued, he grew scared. The old woman had hollow eyes and a sunken mouth; she had a gray tousle of hair, and her body was like a bag of bones.

"Thank you," the old woman said in a squeaky voice, "But for you, I would have to sit in the swamp for thirty three years."

The boy was surprised but did not say a thing. The old lady went on, "The dreariest disaster would happen in the world. People would pray for me like for a blessing…" "Who are you?" the boy asked. "I am Death," the old woman replied. "I am both evil and good. Leaves die in autumn and fall onto the ground; new leaves and flowers sprout in spring. Whatever lives has to die to make room for the young.

It is a law which nobody can break. You need not be afraid of me. Come with me; I will tell you the secret behind any disease, any ailment." "I cannot. My mother is waiting for me," the boy said.

Death grinned and walked along the road. The boy followed her. His feet were walking on their own, totally against his will.

Death brought the boy to the cave where she lived. He spent three long years there.

Death taught him a lot. He learned about all kinds of diseases and how to recognize them. The old woman showed him healing herbs in the forest and in the meadow. He came to know that tormentil was to be dug in autumn, after the grass withered, or in spring, before buds began to show. He learned to make a stomach concoction and burn ointments from the root. He would collect and dry sweet-scented lilac thyme flowers – the herb can sooth a sore throat and stop hardest coughing. Wood anemone can heal toothache; blue angel's eyes are useful to those suffering from bone ache and snake bites. Bladder silene bath can make weak children strong and healthy. In three years, he learned more than can be described.

Once, Death told him, "Today is three years since you pulled me out of the swamp. You may be free. You have mastered the art of healing, but no healer can tell if the remedy will help, if the patient will live or die. Now I have a present for you – you will always know it. If you see me at the bed-foot of an ill man, try and cure him. It I stand at his head, nothing will help him. Now go wherever you want to go and do whatever you please to do."

The young healer did not hesitate to go to his mother. He had missed her badly and worried about her throughout the long years. He did have a reason to be anxious. She nearly cried her heart out when her son was missing; her face grew dark and her body rawboned. Now she was bedridden.

He entered his hut and saw at once that his mother was dying, and Death was standing at her head. The boy cried bitterly and said to himself, "No, I will not let her die. My mother has lived her life in poverty and grief. I want her to see happy days."

He lifted his mother and turned her round so that Death was now at her feet.

The old woman wagged her bony finger at him, "What are you doing, stupid? I will not let you stand in my way." "But she is my mother!" the boy exclaimed.

Death shook her head and vanished.

His mother was so glad to see him back that she soon recovered, and they lived happily together.

The young healer began healing people. He cured many bad illnesses. People knew his eye to be keen and his word to be true – whenever he took on a case, the patient got better. But if he refused, the poor thing was destined to die, and no other healer could save him. He treated both rich and poor folks at no charge – he was happy with whatever people gave him. Soon he was famous all across the country.

Once, he was invited to see a sick widow. He came to her poor hut and saw an exhausted woman. She was lying on the floor, on litter, and small children were pottering around, crying with hunger; his teacher Death was standing at her bedhead.

His heart swelled with pity for the poor children that were to become orphans, and he told Death, "Go away!.." "I cannot," Death replied. "Please have mercy on the children!" "I have neither spite not mercy," Death replied. "I am doing what I am to do." "So I will do what I am to do!" the healer exclaimed and turned the dying woman around; Death was now at her feet.

Death quaked with anger, "You will regret it! You have disobeyed me twice," she turned round and left.

The healer gave the widow a healing concoction, brought some food to the house, bought clothes for the children, and left some money to the family.

A year passed, and a disaster befell the country. A mighty enemy attacked the healer's homeland, setting homes to fire, plundering, and killing everybody in its way. The army was defeated, and the king escaped. A simple soldier, who was a brave man, encouraged the people to stand their ground. He gathered the scattered troops; everybody capable of holding weapons got some; they marched against the enemy.

They defeated the enemy army in a cruel battle, but the leader was wounded badly, and the defender army wavered.

The battle had subsided by the evening. There were only two figures to be seen on the night battlefield – the healer and Death. Whenever the old woman stood at a wounded man's head, the healer walked by, though his heart was breaking. He only helped when Death stood at a soldiers' feet.

At last, they came up to the leader, who was bleeding and lay still, clasping his hands on his chipped sword. The healer bent down to him and heard his heart beating feebly. Raising his eyes, he saw Death at the warrior's head.

"But if he dies," the healer exclaimed, "my homeland will fall. Come whatever may!"

He turned round the wounded man.

Death made a step back and said, "You had it your own way. You neglected the prohibition for the third time. He will live. Now follow me, and I will reveal the final secret to you."

Death brought him to the cave in which he spent three years. She hit the wall, and the rock was split. He could see a stone corridor with endless rows of burning lamps along its walls.

"Look," Death said, "each lamp is the fire of somebody's life." She invited him to go deeper along the corridor.

They stopped in front of four lamps. Three had enough oil in them, and their wicks were smoothly aflame. The fourth lamp was running out of oil, and its blue flame was quivering on the wick, which was nearly dry.

"This is your lamp," Death said, "and those next to it are the lives of the people you took from me. But you rescued me once, so I am going to rescue you. Pour the oil from their lamps into yours, and your life will be long and happy."

Having thought for a while, the healer replied, "I cannot take the life from my mother. Nor can I turn the widow's young children into orphans. I have no right to deprive my homeland of its defender. I will not follow your advice!.."

At that very moment, a tiny flame glinted in his lamp for the last time to go out. The healer fell in a dead faint. Death shrugged her shoulders and returned to her earthly business.

ABOUT A SIMPLE MAN
WHO COMFORTED HIS MASTER

he village headed by the simple man belonged to a most noble gentleman. When the time was ripe for it, the master sent his sons to school, married off his elder daughter, while the younger one, a marriageable girl, stayed with her mother in the family estate. The gentleman won an election and moved to town.

Quite remarkably, many misfortunes came out of the blue when the gentleman was away; his wife died all of a sudden; the estate was nearly burned down; and his younger daughter... Well, her story comes last. It all happened within a week.

The gentleman was enjoying himself in town, totally unaware of what had befallen him. Suddenly, his servant came in to say that his village headman wanted to see the gentleman. The latter ordered to let the simple man in.

The simple man entered the room, made a bow, and scratched his head. Feeling sorry for his master, he wanted to inform the gentleman of his misfortunes without upsetting him too much. So he decided to start by describing the minor misfortunes to prepare his master for the more aggrieving news.

"So, how have you been doing, simple man?" the gentleman asked.

"Alive and kicking," was the answer.

"What is new?"

"I am not sure how to put it, Most Illustrious Master. They say, misfortune, wood, and hair grow throughout the year. Even the priest says that the Lord disciplines the one He loves. Looks like God favors you, Most Illustrious Master. Well, everything is in His hands."

"What are you talking about? Has a misfortune befallen me?"

"It has, Most Illustrious Master. We are all in God's hands. He sent you disappointment, but he also gave you consolation."

"So what is the disappointment?"

"Your penknife, the one your late father gave you, has broken."

"Oh, pest on you! Ahaha! Do you really think a trifle like that can disappoint me? Sure enough, I feel sorry about the knife, for I had it in memory of my father; but what lasts forever? How did they break it?"

"Skinning a hound."

"What? A hound is dead? Which is?"

"All of them are."

"All of them? How come? Such wonderful hounds! Were they ill kept?.."

"Might have been, Most Illustrious Master. But I think it is not the point, for they ate your stallion's meat; and the meat had poison in it—they had prepared it for the wolves."

"So the stallion is dead?" the gentleman shouted, jumping off his chair.

"He is, Most Illustrious Master. The stallion is dead."

"What happened to him? He was a young and healthy horse, just six years old. They must have neglected him, didn't they?"

"Oh Most Illustrious Master, they did not neglect him. But what could they do? For he strained himself."

"Did he? Who dares work him that hard?"

"They could not help it, Most Illustrious Master. They were trying to put out a fire."

"A fire?! How come? Where?"

"The shed caught fire; they began to put it out. They were bringing water in barrels. But what could they do? There was too much work to do—the barn was on fire; the stable was aflame; then it spread to the cowshed..."

"What about the house?"

"The housed had turned to ashes by then. It was the first to catch fire."

"Ay me!" the gentleman lamented, wringing his hands. "So everything has been reduced to ashes, hasn't it?"

"It has, Most Illustrious Master. Ashes."

"Why did the fire start?"

"The house was full of candles; and there was mourning drapery on the windows..."

"You say mourning? Who did they mourn for?"

"Most Illustrious Mistress, your wife..."

"What? Good God, is my wife dead?!"

"Oh yes, Most Illustrious Mistress, she is. May she rest in peace!"

The gentleman was silent. He raised his eyes, which were shedding tears, and said, "God has sent me so many misfortunes. You say He aggrieves, and He consoles. How can He console me now that I have lost so much?"

"Sure He can, Most Illustrious Master! Lord has sent you consolation. The young mistress, your younger daughter, has given birth to a baby..."

PEOPLE GETTING RICH

In a village, there lived a poor man. Even though he worked his fingers to the bone and never wasted his money, he failed to get rich. Whatever he did, poverty was like a nasty guest in his home.

Once, Saint Peter was riding on horseback past the village. He was heading for Heaven on business, and stopped by the inn to feed his horse. Having learned about it, folks came running to Saint Peter so that he could deliver their requests to God. The poor man came, too, asking Saint Peter to find out why he was so poor in spite of his diligent work and decent life. At first, Saint Peter refused, saying that he had a lot to do and could easily forget about the request. But the poor man begged him so wildly that the saint felt sorry for him; he took the gold saddle with gold stirrups off his horse's back and gave it to him, saying, "Keep it till I am back. When in Heaven, I will notice that my saddle is missing; it will remind me your request. I'll pick it on my way back."

Having said it, Saint Peter departed; the peasant hid the gold saddle with gold stirrups in his lumber room and waited for the saint to come and bring news from Heaven impatiently.

Finally, Saint Peter completed whatever work he had in Heaven, and began preparing his horse for the return journey. That was the moment he noticed that the saddle was missing, and remembered the poor man and his request. He came back to God and asked him what made the man dog poor in spite of his hard work and honesty.

"It is his not being a deceitful fraud what makes him poor," the Lord said.

As soon as Saint Peter's figure could be seen at a distance, the peasant ran to meet him, eager to know what had kept him from getting rich. Saint Peter recognized him at once and shouted to him, "Bring me the saddle; I will be traveling on!" "Did the Lord tell you what keeps me from becoming rich?" the man asked before he ran to fetch the saddle. He could not overcome curiosity. "It is your not being a fraud," the saint said. "Now do fetch my saddle!"

The peasant was no fool; he was a quick learner. So he decided not to give the saddle back to the saint. He feigned surprise and asked, "What saddle are you talking about? I have no saddle." "What are you talking about? Have you forgotten? When on my way to the Kingdom of Heaven, I gave you my saddle to keep. Please hurry and bring it!" "I think it was not me whom you gave your saddle."

The saint was in a great hurry and could not afford the time; he waved his hand and traveled on. So the man got a gold saddle with gold stirrups quite effortlessly.

"Let us see what comes next," the peasant thought and went to the dealer to sell his trophy. After the usual negotiation, they agreed on a price of a hundred guldens and a cow. The dealer provided the money immediately and promised to bring the cow to the peasant as soon as it returned from the pasture. That was the moment he would get the saddle.

In the evening, the dealer brought the cow and demanded the saddle. But the peasant said, "No, I will not give you the saddle for the cow alone." "Why? I have already given you a hundred guldens!" "What are you talking about? When was it? Who saw it? Take your cow and go away, leave me alone!"

So the peasant pocketed the money, but he did not get away with that—the dealer sued him, and the judge appointed a trial. When the trial day came, the peasant went to the inn and sat there. People asked him why he would not go to court. "How can I appear in court without a coat?" he replied. "I can lend you mine," a man said, taking off his fur coat and giving it to the peasant.

The peasant put on the coat but did not move. They asked him why he was not leaving for court, for it was high time he did. "Can't you see that I have no boots? How can I enter the court barefoot?" "Take mine and do go," another man said, taking off his boots and giving them to the artful man.

He put on the boots but kept sitting, saying that he had no hat. He did not leave until somebody gave him a hat. The three man who had given him clothing said, "Let us go and see the trial."

They did.

The dealer told the story as it was and demanded a hundred guldens back. But the peasant would not admit it. "You see, Your Honor," he said, "I am so unfortunate that everybody is robbing me; everybody is trying to fleece me. I own nothing; I work for people; but they want to strip me off my last money. For instance, this man would claim the coat I am wearing to be his," he said pointing at the one who had lent his fur coat to him.

"It is!" the man shouted.

"Here you are, Your Honor!" the artful man went on. "The one next to him could pull my boots off my feet!"

He pointed at the owner of the boots, and the letter replied, "The boots are mine, Your Honor!"

"Here you are!" the accused exclaimed. "I am pretty sure the third one could tear my hat off my head." He pointed at the one who had lent him the hat.

"Don't you lie! The hat is mine!"

The befuddled judge believed that everybody had agreed to rob the peasant in broad daylight. He sent the dealer and the rest away, and declared the peasant not guilty. He had everything — the gold saddle with gold stirrups, the fur coat, the boots, and the hat. He began getting rich, as he played cunning all the time.

DO WIVES LIKE THIS EXIST?

Once upon a time, there were a peasant and his wife. They seemed to be ill-starred, and everything was topsy-turvy for them. They even had to sell their only cow.

As the peasant was taking the cow to the market, he met another peasant on horseback. "Where are you taking your cow?" "To the fair. I have no fodder for her." "Look, let me give you my horse for your cow."

The peasant gave him the cow, took the horse, and went on. He met a peasant who was taking a swine to the fair. He said, "Your horse is blind and thin. A crock of a horse. My swine is fat; it will have piglets; you will sell them and climb out of poverty. Let us exchange them!"

The peasant did not hesitate to agree. After a short while, another peasant with a ewe caught up with him. They talked for a while, and the ewe's owner said, "Your swine is too thin; it would be a great deal of trouble to plump it. The ewe would give you fleece at once. Let us exchange them!"

The peasant agreed again. As he walked on, he came across another peasant carrying a goose in a bag. He said, "Hey, give me the ewe and have the goose. You will have three dozen eggs and a proper flock of geese. You will get rich. What good is a single ewe?"

The peasant admired his speech. He exchanged the ewe for the goose and walked on.

"Listen, brother, why drag the goose about?" a peasant carrying a cock said to him. "Take the cock for it. He crows every hour; you can use him as a clock, which is much fun. Your goose is no fun, is it?"

They exchanged their birds. The peasant took the cock and went to the fair.

Evening came, and he felt hungry. There was an inn nearby, but he had nothing to pay with. So he had to give the cock to the innkeeper. Sitting in the inn, the peasant told his story, "I have had a great deal of trading today. I exchanged a cow for a crock of a horse, the horse for a swine, the swine for a ewe, the ewe for a goose, the goose for a cock. What I get for the cock is a supper."

A rich gentleman was enjoying himself in the inn. Listening to the peasant's story, he said with a smile, "Is that what you call trade? I wonder what your wife will say." "She will not say a thing. Whatever I do, she does not mind. We never fight." "I wish I could see it with my own eyes! I think no wife in this world could keep from beating the tar out of her husband for such trading. Let me go with you to see what happens."

The two of them went to the peasant's house. The gentleman stood at the door to listen, and the peasant came in and told his wife about his unfortunate trading. His wife said, "Thanks God you have come back unscathed. The loss is no big deal. If nobody ever made a loss, there would be no trade at all."

Hearing it, the gentleman threw a purse full of money to the peasant and said before he left, "Have it as a gift for living without quarrels. I wish all wives were like this!"

THE OWL AND THE HAWK

The Lord ordered that the Hawk should feed on small birds. The Owl was terrified to learn it, for the hawk could hunt her owlets.

So she invited him to an inn to wine and dine him. Having done so, she begged, "Don't you touch my children." "Which are yours?" the Hawk asked. "The prettiest ones are mine," the Owl said. "Alright," the Hawk said.

Once the Hawk went hunting. Whatever nestlings he saw were pretty. Finally, he came across the owlets. "These are the ugliest creatures ever," he said and ate them.

To make matters worse, other birds came to know what the Owl had said, and laughed at her.

The owl has ceased to fly in the daytime since then. Ashamed, she hides from their cruel jokes.

THE REASON WHY
THE HARE EATS NO MEAT

Once upon a time, it was not only the Hare who ate no meat. The Fox would feed on buds and leaves alone. The Wolf came to visit him and said, "What a foul life you lead, fellow, munching on buds and sucking on tree branches. Be my student. I will teach you to be a butcher; and you will eat meat and liver every day."

"What am I to do?" the Fox asked. "At first, you will have no duties but to follow my orders. You will see what comes then."

The Fox agreed eagerly and joined the Wolf. They walked, and walked, and came to a grassy sweep to see a horse grazing.

They hid in the shrubs. The Wolf said, "Stand in front of me and tell me if you can see my eyes glowing."

The Fox did so and said, "I can. They are glowing like embers."

The Wolf asked, "Look, is my hair bristled?"

"It is. It is awfully bristled," the Fox answered.

The Wolf asked again, "Does my tail wriggle fast?"

The Fox looked and said, "As fast as a whip!"

"So take it away!" the Wolf shouted, leaping at the horse, and tore his stomach open. The Fox joined him. They tore the horse to pieces and ate him.

When the Wolf and the Fox grew hungry again, they killed a ram; then they killed a cow.

It occurred to the Fox that he had become an experienced butcher and could do without the wolf; so he went hunting by himself.

He came across the little Hare biting on buds and leaves in the shrubs.

"How stupid you are to feed on greens alone!" the Fox told him. "Meat tastes so much better and gives so much more energy. If you ate meat, you would become stronger than the largest dog. Let me teach you how to be a butcher."

"What am I to do?" the Hare asked.

"At first, you will only have to do what I tell you."

The Hare liked the idea; so he joined the Fox. Soon, they came to a grassy sweep to see a horse grazing. The fox hid in the shrubs and told the Fox, "Go and tell me if you can see my eyes glowing." "They are glowing like embers!" the Hare answered. "Is my hair bristled?" "Oh, awfully bristled!" "Now tell me if my tail is wriggling." "It is, just like branches in the wind," the Hare said in a squeaky voice." "So the time has come!" the Fox shouted and attacked the horse. But the horse noticed the Fox and kicked him dead with his hoof.

Seeing it, the Hare quivered with fear and thought, "I would rather munch on buds, grass, and leaves than be kicked with a hoof!"

The Hare has not touched meat since then, not a chance.

THE DOG'S WINTER THOUGHTS AND SUMMER THOUGHTS

I n winter, when the frost is bitter, the Dog curls up, covering his body with his tail, shivers and thinks, "I cannot wait for summer to come! I will surely build a kennel, at least a small and rickety one!"

As soon as summer comes, the Dog mellows in the sunshine, stretching his legs, his tail loose. Stretching and looking around, he says, "I would have to build a very large kennel. That would be a great deal of trouble! No need to bother. I can do without it!"

IS THERE JUSTICE IN THIS WORLD?

Once, a peasant went to the forest to get some firewood. It was raining cats and dogs; the wind was uprooting pine trees.

The peasant came to the forest and began to cut branches. All of a sudden, he heard somebody moaning complainingly. The peasant's heart leapt into his boots. Yet, he came to where the moans seemed to be coming from. He saw a bear pinned down to the ground by a fallen pine tree. He could barely breathe.

The peasant felt sorry for the animal. He fetched a long stick and two logs. Using the stick to lift the pine tree a little, he placed its butt-end on a log. Then he lifted the other end and placed it on the other log, releasing the Bear.

Having collected his wits, the Bear said, "I am going to eat you!" "Of all the nerve!" the peasant answered. "I have saved you from certain death! You should be grateful to me. How dare you!"

The Bear insisted that he would eat the peasant. The man tried to escape, but failed—the Bear caught him.

Things looked black to the peasant. So he spoke to the Bear, "You cannot eat anybody without a trial. Let somebody judge."

The Bear agreed. They went in search of a judge. The weather grew even nastier—there was a howling gale and a downpour. Suddenly, they saw the Horse munching on oak branches in the woods.

"Please set the argument for us," the peasant told the horse.

The man told it as it was. The Horse answered, "The Bear is right. You always get evil for the good you do. When I was young, I did not spare myself working for my owner. Now that I am old and weak, he has no straw for me. Look at the nasty weather! He sent me to the woods to munch on oak branches."

The peasant did not like what the horse said. "Let us find another judge," he told the Bear.

They walked on until they came across the Hare.

"Hey, puss," said the Bear, "set the argument for us." The Hare was afraid, "How can I judge you?" The peasant told it as it was. The Hare said, "You always get evil for doing good. I have never done anything to anybody, but everyone attacks me—the dog, and the wolf, and even the crow. I cannot take it anymore. I am going to drown myself."

The Hare could have drowned but for the Toad, who was sitting by the water. Seeing the hare, she leaped away in terror. "Aha," the Hare thought, "there is no need to drown myself yet. There are creatures who are still afraid of me."

The peasant and the man walked on. They came across the Fox.

They told the whole thing as it was. "Set the argument for us, will you?" "I will," the Fox agreed.

The peasant took the Fox aside and whispered to him, "If you judge us the right way, I will give you six hens." The Fox said with a nod, "How can I judge you without seeing the place the Bear was caught?"

The three of them came to see the broken pine tree.

"You say you lifted the pine?" the Fox said in a surprised voice. "It is impossible!"

The peasant used the stick to lift the pine tree.

"Now," the Fox said, "you Bear get under the tree to show me the way you were lying."

The Bear got under the tree, and the peasant took the stick away. The pine tree pinned the Bear down to the ground again.

The peasant said thank you to the Fox and gave him a hen to start with.

On the following day, the Fox came to get a second hen, and then he came for a third one. The peasant did not contradict; but on the fourth day, he borrowed a gun from his neighbor and lay by the henhouse on the watch for the Fox. Seeing the Fox, he shot.

The shot was poor; the Fox broke into a run, shouting back, "So this is what you give me for doing good, peasant!"

The end.

MAZEK'S DEBT

A peasant whose name was Mazek bought a horse from a Gypsy at a fair. He liked the horse greatly; but he was a penny short. The Gypsy would not rebate. So Mazek had to borrow it from his relative Jazek.

"When are you going to pay me back, Mazek?" Jazek asked.

"On Easter day," Mazek replied.

Jazek agreed to give him a penny. Mazek bought the horse, and they went home.

Easter came, and Jazek went to Mazek to get his penny back. Seeing him at a distance, approaching, Mazek rushed to his wife, ordering her to tell Jazek that he was dead. Barefooted as he was, he lay on a bench in the lumber room, holding his breath. When Jazek entered the house, Mazek's wife said her husband to be dead.

"So where is the dead man?" Jazek asked. "I think I need to see him before he is buried."

Mazek's wife took Jazek to the lumber room and pointed at the dead man lying on the bench.

"But why have you not washed his feet? They are so dirty," Jazek said and grabbed a bucket of cold water to pour it onto Mazek's feet.

Mazek pulled his leg with a gasp.

"Aha!" Jazek said. "Quite dead, aren't you, Mazek? Give me my penny, for it is what I came for." "Please forgive me," Mazek replied. "I do not have a penny to repay my debt.

I was going to die of grief." "When are you going to give it back, Mazek?" Jazek asked. "Come on Saint John's Day," Mazek answered.

Saint John's Day came. Jazek was going to visit Mazek again and get his penny back. But Mazek prepared in advance. He told his wife, "We are going to make a fool of him this time."

He ordered her to take him to the cemetery in a coffin and put him into a grave. He said, "Cover the grave with boards so that I can get out."

When Jazek came, Mazek's wife told him that her husband was in the cemetery.

"Dearest relative, please show me his grave. I should pray for the deceased," Jazek said. Surely enough, he knew what it was about.

When at the cemetery, he came up to the grave and began cracking tree branches, stamping his feet, jumping, and roaring like an ox. "Make the ox go away, Kasia, for he will fall down on me, Heaven forbid!" "Aha, quite dead you are, aren't you?" Jazek said, taking the boards off the grave. "You outfox me again," Mazek said. "But what can I do? I have no penny. I had to be on the dodge." "So when are you going to pay me back?" Jazek asked. "Come on Saint Michael's Day. I will pay you back, by God."

Saint Michael's Day came; yet Mazek had no penny. He made up his mind to play the game again. When Jazek came for his penny, Mazek's wife told him that her husband was really dead that time, and that he was lying in the empty chapel near the forest. Jazek wanted to see the deceased for the last time, so Mazek's wife told him the way. It was a long way to go.

When Jazek arrived, it was getting dark. Peeping at the door, he saw his relative lying in a coffin in the middle of the chapel. He stood there waiting for the dead man to move. All of a sudden, robbers appeared from the woods—one, three, ten of them!—and sneaked into the chapel, lit candles, and began to divide the profits. Finally, everything was divided but for a saber.

"There is no dividing it," their chieftain said. "Let the one who cuts off the dead man's head in a single blow have it."

The robbers muttered. One was afraid of dead men; another said that the dead man would come to him in his dreams; yet another claimed sabering dead men to be a sin. Shortly speaking, everyone refused but for one. He took the saber, approached the coffin, and tried different blows to find the best way to cut off Mazek's head. Suddenly, Mazek jumped, sitting up in his coffin, and cried blue murder.

"Hey, robbers, brothers, lost souls, come help me!"

That moment Jazek began making noise, banging his fists on the rotten boards; the robbers got scared and took to their heels, leaving their plunder behind them.

They ran away; Jazek entered the chapel to greet Mazek. Mazek said, "Let us divide the plunder. There is plenty for both of us."

They did divide the costly things; Jazek got the saber. Looking at the two similar heaps, Jazek said with a sigh, "Fine. But you owe me a penny."

One of the robbers, who was the bravest and the most curious one, came up to the chapel to see what was going on in there. He popped his head in at the door and saw the two dividing the plunder. Thinking them to be sinful dead men, he froze with fear right at the door. Mazek saw his head and leapt at him, grabbing the hat he was wearing. He threw the hat angrily at Jazek. "Here you are!" he shouted, "Keep the hat, for it does cost a penny!"

Terrified to death, the robber ran to his band. "The dead men are dividing our plunder and fighting," he said. "They tried to tear my head off and grabbed my hat—I barely escaped!"

VERY WORST PUNISHMENT

A rich landowner had a son; the son would not get married, claiming early marriage to be no good. His father insisted, saying a single landowner to be of little worth—they say, three corners of the house rest on the mistress, and only one rests on the master. "Moreover," he said, "one should marry young; late marriage is Devil's delight."

Finally, the father reasoned his son into marriage.

The poor thing was unlucky enough to take a wicked, peevish, and quarrelsome witch of a woman for his wife. She could hardly manage the housekeeping but was very eager to command everybody. Whatever her husband brought she took out. They would fight and quarrel over every trifle. The husband developed a habit of sneaking out of the house as soon as he could feel a storm approaching. He would not come until late at night.

Once in early spring, the father and son were ploughing a land plot of theirs in the woods. The father brought an ox of his, and the son brought one of his. They harnessed both to do it faster. At noon, they went home for lunch, leaving the oxen in the woods.

The two men returned in the afternoon to see no oxen. They rummaged the woods until they found half a tail, a head, and hooves along with guts scattered around. They realized it was a wolf who had done it. They traced the bandit and found it in the thick woods; it was too full to move. The men tied it up and stopped to think of the worst punishment possible.

The father said, "Let us get its tail caught in a split log to make it die of hunger."

"It is no punishment," his son said, "we had better make it marry. That would be the very worst punishment."

MARIA: WHAT IS DESTINED TO COME SHALL COME

Once upon a time, a rich prince was living his last years peacefully in his castle. He had an only son, who was a handsome and strong knight, widely famous for his courage and valor. But the old princess wanted to have a daughter. So she asked the prince to adopt an orphan. They did and never regretted doing so, for the girl grew to be kind and obedient, and everybody liked her. Her name was Maria.

Once, a dusted messenger appeared in the castle to say that the king had waged war on the infidels and wanted everyone capable of holding weapons to join his troops. Brave warriors set out on the march. The old prince, sick and weak as he was, sent his son to join the army.

The young knight led his henchmen to the battlefield. Their chain mails were shining like the sun; and their swords were flashing like the lightning.

On the road stood a gray-haired gusli player, singing songs and telling fortunes. The prince's son stopped to find out what was ahead of him, for war is no children's game. The old man looked at the palm of his hand and said, "Your Grace, your life will be happy—you will be distinguished in the war, come home famous and unhurt, and marry a nice girl. Yet she will be not a noble girl but a poor orphan kindly reared."

The knight threw a gold coin to the musician, spurred on his horse, and traveled on.

The war was long; much blood was spilt; many warriors fell. As soon as it was over, the king gave the prince's son a generous reward for having fought courageously and killed many infidels, and let him go home, famous and honored as he was. When the prince's son approached his father's castle, the old prince and princess came out to meet him. So did their foster daughter, whom they had come to love as if she was their own child. The young warrior jumped off his horse, kissed his father's hand, then his mother's hand; but he did not even look at Maria. He thought of what the gusli player had said, and it occurred to him, "Everything he foretold has come true so far. I wonder if he predicted the girl to become my wife."

His fame went to his head, and he grew proud, as it often happens to young men; he came to hate Maria and made up his mind to send her away.

Maria had grown to be a paragon—beautiful and smart, bright as a star and meek as a dove. Seeing the prince's son, handsome and stately, she fell in love with him at once. The more angrily he looked at her, the more she liked him—it is always that way with girls.

Once, the young knight ordered his devoted slave to set afloat a boat with no oars or rudder with a little food in it. Early in the morning, he invited Maria to stroll along the riverbank, had the girl get into the boat, and pushed it far to the middle of the river.

The stream was carrying the boat on and on very swiftly. At first Maria wrang her hands and cried; then she fell asleep, exhausted and distressed. At night, the boat was stuck under a watermill wheel.

In the morning, the miller pushed the stone aside and let the water run, but the wheel would not turn. He went to see if a sawyer was stuck there and suddenly saw a boat with a beautifully dressed girl sleeping inside it. He called his wife, and the two of them carried her into their house. When Maria woke up, she told her sad story. The miller and his wife were kind people. They pitied the poor orphan and let her stay with them. Maria was a diligent and dexterous girl. She helped them about the house; and soon the mill shone like a palace.

Once, Maria took a small boat to go to the forest on the opposite bank for firewood. All of a sudden, she heard a hunting horn and a patter of hooves. Looking out of the shrubs, the girl saw the prince's son galloping towards her. He had been hunting there with his people. The poor girl ran right through the woods. But the knight noticed and recognized her. He was angry to see her in his way again, for he had hoped that she had either drowned or been taken far away by the river. He ordered his slaves to catch the girl. They started after her, but she ran like a scared deer until she could hide at a swamp. The slaves came back with their clothes torn and their faces scratched.

When it was getting dark, Maria wandered out. She did not dare return to the mill for the fear of the prince's son coming there for her. She went on and on through the dark woods, all night long, and found herself in a vast field at dawn. Far ahead, she saw towers of a castle and headed for them. She finally reached the fence of a beautiful garden with colorful flowerbeds. She saw twelve girls among the flowers, wearing festive dresses, tambouring with gold and silver threads. They were the local prince's daughters.

Maria made a low bow to them and asked for some bread and shelter. Judging by her speech and costly dress, though torn, the princesses recognized her to be a noble girl who had seen better days. The princesses felt sorry for the poor girl and asked their father to let her stay in the castle.

Days passed. Once Maria did tambouring too, and her embroidery made everybody gasp in delight. They asked her about her origin and what had brought her there. Maria told them her sad story as it was. The kind princesses could not help crying as they heard it. They hugged Maria and told her not to grieve anymore, for she would be their thirteenth sister, and they would not let anybody hurt her. They dressed Maria in costly garments and invited her to dine with them. She became their sworn sister.

The poor orphan was enjoying days of delight again. But she never forgot the prince's son; even though he had hurt her so badly, she missed him and cried secretly.

She spent many days playing and having fun. Once, a messenger arrived to tell them a young knight was coming with his people to propose to one of the prince's daughter. Having heard it, Maria got scared and asked her friends to hide her. The princesses took their sworn sister to the highest tower of the castle and promised that none of them would marry the cruel son of the prince.

The local prince and his wife gave the guests a warm welcome and said that they were prepared to let their daughter marry the prince if she wanted to. The knight looked at the girls, and saw that each was pretty and could be a good wife for him.

He talked pleasantly to the eldest one, sighing and boasting about his wealth and glory; but she pretended to hear nothing and understand nothing—she was as cold as stone. When the prince's son proposed to her, she rejected him. The young knight grew angry, for he had not expected to get the gate.

On the following day, the young man tried his luck with the second sister, but the answer was the same. Every day, the young man tried to coax a daughter of the prince's, but it was to no avail. The prince's son stayed in the castle for twelve days. When the youngest sisters refused to marry him, he went green with anger, jumped on his horse's back and rushed out of the castle without saying goodbye. He was followed by long-faced matchmakers and slaves, looking perplexed and ashamed, for it seemed impossible to return without a wife.

At noon, the unhappy matchmakers stopped to have a rest in the woods near a half-ruined small chapel, in which lived a monk who was nearly blind and deaf. The young knight was restless—he just could not come home without a wife! He had promised his parents to bring them a daughter-in-law. The rumor about his wedding had traveled around the country. He was going to be ridiculous.

"One of them will be my wife even if I have to force her!" he made up his mind and ordered his servants to return to the castle and kidnap one of the princesses.

The slaves went there to execute their young lord's order. They reached the castle in the twilight. It was then that Maria went to the garden for a walk. She had stayed in the tower for twelve days in a row.

The slaves waylaid her, caught her, stopped her mouth, and took her away. They got to the chapel at night. Everything was ready for the faithless wedding by that time—a priest in his orarion was standing by the altar lit up by two small candles.

Hearing the patter of hooves, the prince's son rushed to meet his slaves, grabbed the girl, who was still hardly conscious with fear, and brought her into the chapel without even looking at her face. The monk married them in a hurry, as they always do in such cases, and the matchmakers went home relieved. The prince's son put his bride on horseback behind himself and disappeared into the dark.

In the morning, a messenger told the old prince and the princess that the newlyweds were coming. Traditionally, everybody came out to the castle gate to treat the newly married couple to bread and salt. They beat drums and played music, and a great crowd gathered.

The wedding train arrived. The matchmakers handed the bride to the groom, who nearly dropped her at seeing whom he had brought home. Maria threw her at her foster parents' feet. They were very happy and surprised, since they had long believed her to be dead. They forced Maria to stand up and began to hug and kiss her.

The young knight realized that he could not escape his destiny. He gave his bride a closer look, and scales seemed to have fallen from his eyes. Maria appeared to be the prettiest of all beauties. He regretted being so cruel to the orphan, put off his pride, and went to his knees, asking the girl to forgive him. Maria forgave him from the bottom of her heart; for she had always loved him.

They had a merry wedding. Noble guests came from all around the country. The twelve daughters of the neighbor prince came too, bringing costly presents to their sworn sister. When the feast was over and the guests had left, the newlyweds began their life together in the old prince's castle. They lived to be very old and never said a single nasty word to each other.

IT DOES NOT STAB, NOR DOES IT SHOOT, YET IT KNOCKS ONE SENSELESS

Once upon a time, four mares and a colt were grazing on a meadow at evening time. The Wolf appeared from the woods nearby, and the colt caught his attention.

The colt noticed the Wolf and hid behind the mares. The Wolf tried to come closer, but the mares kicked their legs desperately. Seeing the shiny horseshoes, the Wolf dared not approach the horses. A worker came and saw the horses anxious. He did not see the Wolf; yet he gathered the horses and brought them home. Even the colt kept up with their trot.

The Wolf grew angry. To miss a colt! He made up his mind to sneak into the stables and eat the colt right there. So said so done. By the time the worker was letting the horses into the stables, one by one, the Wolf had hidden under the crib. The worker locked the door and left to have a supper. Having finished his meal, he was preparing to go to bed. Walking by the stables, he heard the horses wheeze and kick their legs violently. The worker returned to the house and told his master, "Something must be wrong. I could hardly quiet the horses on my way home. They looked scared. The colt was sticking to them, too. Now they are wheezing and kicking their legs so violently that I am afraid to approach the stables."

The master knew he was in trouble. He lit a torch, took a boot, entered the stables, locking the door behind him, and felt for the robber—to find the Wolf under the crib! The master dragged the Wolf out by his tail and hit him with the boot. The Wolf collapsed, looking lifeless. The master saw the Wolf to be dead. He threw him out of the door and started rummaging the stables for another. He was a smart man but made a slip. The Wolf was alive.

Dragging his feet in the woods, he came across a Lion. "Where are you going?" "Nowhere in particular." "Let us go together."

The two of them came across a Bear.

"Where are you going?" the Lion asked. "Nowhere in particular." "Let us go together."

The three of them encountered a Boar.

"Where are you going?" "Nowhere in particular." "Let us go together."

They walked until they saw a beech grove in a valley. They sat down, and the Lion said, "Let everyone show what he can do."

The Lion uprooted a beech tree with his paw. The Boar lifted one with his tushes and fell it. The Bear climbed another beech tree and began breaking its branches and scattering them around.

"Your turn, Wolf," the Lion said.

But the Wolf could do nothing of the kind. He tried to pull the wool over their eyes. "Lord! You are great at what you do, but please listen to my story. I was going to slaughter a colt; I sneaked into the stables; but all of a sudden, the master came with a heavy thing and grabbed me by the tail. The thing does not stab, nor does it shoot, but it does knock one senseless. I fainted. He threw me out of the door like a dog; I could hardly reach this place. He is the one who is masterful!"

The Lion asked the Wolf, "Do you know the master?" "I do. I know him well. He rides by on his way to the fair every Wednesday." "So show him to me. I will try my strength against his."

The Wolf jumped back and exclaimed, "God forbid! I will not survive it!" "Show him from a distance," the Lion said. "Why not," the Wolf agreed.

The fair opened. The Wolf made a lair close enough to the road to point at the man when he is passing by and hide quickly. They sat there on the watch for him. Folks were coming to the fair, driving their cattle, horses, and hogs. At last, the master appeared. The Wolf jumped up to the Lion, "Coming!" he said and disappeared into his lair so that the man could not see him.

The Lion came out of his hide and spoke as follows, "Listen, man. They say you are ever so strong. Let us match our strengths."

Seeing the Lion, the Bear, and the Boar facing him, the man replied, "How can we match our strength with no special equipment? Wait a little. I will bring some on my way back from the fair."

The Lion, the Bear, and the Boar stayed in the woods, and the master went to the fair, racking his brains to invent a way to catch all the three animals. Returning from the fair, he saw them waiting for him. The man told the Lion, "Send one of you to help me fetch the equipment. We will start as soon as we bring it." "Which one?" the Lion asked. "The Boar is strong but awkward. The Bear is a simple lad. He will cope with it." "Alright. Let the Bear come with you."

The man took the Bear. They came to the man's yard, where a huge stone was lying near the stables. The man had brought it in winter to build a bridge later. He pointed at the stone to the Bear, "Carry it to the forest."

He went to have lunch.

The Bear tried every possible way to lift the stone. It appeared too heavy. The Bear came to the master and said, "There is no way I can lift it."

The master grinned, "If you cannot carry it, why match my strength against you?" "I can carry it alright. I have a strong back. Just help me shoulder it."

The master called the worker. They took thick sticks; the Bear turned his back to them. They lifted the stone onto his shoulders. The poor thing died without making a sound. The master lit a pipe, put some sausage under his armpit, grabbed a stick, and headed for the woods. Seeing him, the Lion asked where the Bear and the equipment were. The master said, "He has fallen behind me. Must be short of breath. I think he will be here soon."

He sat on a tree stub, took out his sausage and enjoyed his meal. As the Lion smelled the sausage, he felt hungry and asked the master for a piece of it. The master gave him some. The Lion liked it greatly. "What is it made of?" he asked. Pointing at the Boar, the master whispered to him, "Kill him, and I will make you as much sausage as you like."

The Lion came up to the Boar and hit him dead with his paw. The master took to work. He gutted the Boar. Seeing fat, the Lion picked some on his claw and ate it. The master flicked him on the forehead. "Wait until I make sausage. I have to skin the body, blowtorch it, and broil the sausage before you can eat it." "I cannot wait," the Lion said. "You would have to tie me up."

The man went to the woodcutters, got an axe, fell a birch tree, cut a thick wedge, ordered the Lion to stand with his face to a beech tree, and started to wedge behind his back. He wedged and wedged for a while and suddenly hit the Lion's head.

The Lion roared. The Wolf leaped out of his lair and said, "What did I tell you? It does not stab, nor does it shoot, but it does knock one senseless!" He rushed into the woods.

The master sent for a wagon to bring the carcasses of the Lion and the Boar home. He did give a lavish feast.

ABOUT A RICH GENTLEMAN

Once upon a time, there was a rich gentleman. He had plenty of money, which he would hide in an old willow hollow. When the hollow was full to the brim, the gentleman said, "Whatever happens will be no skin off my nose. Even if my house burns down, I am not afraid. My money is safe."

As soon as he said it, a thunderstorm broke out; a lightning struck the gentleman's estate and burned it down to ashes. To crown it all, a river flood washed the willow away. The gentleman lost everything and had to beg for food.

The willow arrived at a peasant's yard. How would he know about the money hidden in the hollows? The willow lay in his backyard. It was totally useless until the peasant's plough was broken. He came up to the willow tree, hit it with an axe, and the money spattered out of the hollow. The peasant collected it and became rich at once.

After several years, a dog poor beggar came to him to stay overnight. It was the gentleman who had hid his money in the hollow. The peasant talked to him and found out that his guest used to be rich, too, but called down the wrath of God, and the money willow was gone.

The peasant told the story to his wife secretly. Seeing that the beggar had nothing but breadcrumbs in his bag, his wife said, "Give me your bread crumbs. I will bake you some fresh bread."

The beggar gave her the stale bread; and she baked a loaf with a lot of money inside. The old man thanked her and traveled on.

Once, he came across some workers driving hogs. He sold the bread to them for a red cent. The workers came to their master, showed him the bread, and the master recognized it.

Several more years passed. The dog poor beggar came to the master's yard again. The master wanted to help him by putting a purse full of money on the bridge. He got under the bridge to make sure it was the wanderer who got the money. While approaching the bridge, the beggar was thinking about what would come of him if he grew blind. He closed his eyes and walked blindly, feeling for obstacles with his stick. He crossed the bridge without noticing the money.

The master got from under the bridge, picked the purse, and never tried to help the beggar anymore. If his fate was punishing him for being too proud, there was no way he could help.

HOW A SMITH WORKED HIS WAY TO HEAVEN

nce upon a time, there was a smith. He led a merry life and was good for nothing. But suddenly he felt his death approaching and told his apprentice, "Listen. When I die, put a hammer and a couple of long sharp nails into my coffin."

The apprentice did so. They buried the smith. The smith came up to the gate of Heaven and asked Saint Peter to let him in. But he objected, "You have sinned a lot. I cannot let you in. Walk on."

The smith walked on and came to hell. Gatekeepers were nowhere to be seen; the gate was locked. The smith took his hammer and banged at the door. The demons woke up and sent one to find out what the noise was.

Hardly had the demon opened the gate and popped his head out when the smith grabbed him by the ear and nailed it to the pillar on his right.

The demon shrieked with pain. The rest heard him and sent another demon to see why the first one was making so much noise. As soon as the second demon appeared, the smith grabbed him and nailed him to the pillar on his left. The two demons screamed so desperately that the Head of the Demons got up and said, "I am going to see what has happened."

The Head of the Demons stuck his head out. The smith very nearly caught him and nailed him to a pillar, too, but the Head of the Demons jumped back and shut the gate close. He shut the gate close and ran to God through the backdoor. He said, "There is a smith at my gate. He has already nailed two of my demons to the gate by their ears; I hardly escaped. You must take him to Heaven. If we let him in, I refuse to rule hell anymore."

God was reluctant to take the smith to Heaven, but the demon insisted, "I will not leave until you have taken him to Heaven."

God cannot have a demon in his Kingdom, can he? So he had to take the smith to Heaven.

ABOUT A PRINCE
WHO DID NOT WANT TO DIE

A king had an only son. Once, the son told his father, "Father, we are overwhelmingly wealthy; and still we are to die. Give me a soldier of yours, and I will go to a place where people do not die."

His father agreed. The prince and the soldier wandered through the thick woods until they saw three robbers. The robbers had a horse to ride you on clouds, an invisibility cloak, a diamond watch, and a diamond ball. The prince came up to them, and they spoke to him, "Please judge which of us should have the ball." The prince said, "Alright. I am going to throw the ball as far as I can. Run for it. The one who gets it first will keep it."

The robbers agreed. When the prince threw the ball, the robbers ran as fast as their legs could carry them to get it. One of them had a bad fall and died; another fell and kicked the bucket, too; the third fell down and passed out.

The prince found the ball, gave it to the soldier, and ordered that he should take it to the king and never come back. He got onto the horse, flung on the cloak, put the watch in his pocket, and said to the horse, "Bring me to the place where people do not die."

The horse flew up into the sky. They galloped for two days and finally reached the kingdom in which people do not die.

The local king had a daughter. The prince liked her; so the two of them got married. They lived peacefully for a while;

but the prince grew homesick. He told his wife, "I am going to visit my father and be back soon." His wife replied, "Do not go. How can you get there?" But he was stubborn, "Be quiet, stupid woman! If I could reach this place, I can easily come back."

He mounted his horse and left.

Having reached his father's kingdom, he saw nothing but water and stones. Straining his eyes and ears, he could finally make out his former slave saying to his former maid, "Where has our master been?" She replied, "Demons must have taken him to hell."

Hearing it, the prince descended from the clouds to slap the maid on the face for talking nonsense. But it was not the maid. Death had assumed her appearance. Seeing him descending to the ground, Death said, "Aha, so you have shown up, dear! I got you!"

The prince was dead in a moment. His horse returned to the prince's wife. She saw the horse and burst into tears, "Something awful must have happened! The horse is here, but my husband has not come."

She mounted the horse and galloped to the woods where her husband had died. Seeing him dead, she grieved so heavily that soon died, too. The horse came back to the kingdom where people do not die, to live until hard work broke his wind.

ANUSZKA THE GOLDEN BRAID

Once upon a time, there was a family with eleven children. A twelfth was born—a daughter. Everybody in the village was the godfather or the godmother to one of the children; but the family could not find godparents for the twelfth girl. The father said, "I'll go out and ask the first passers-by to be the baby's godparents.

So said, so done. The first person he came across was a sorceress. He stayed away from her. Seeing an old couple sitting on a bench, he came up to them and asked them to come to his daughter's baptismal on Sunday.

The sorceress said, "Aha! You did not want me to be your daughter's godmother. You are going to have a rough time with her. She will have hard luck." But the old couple said, "She will have a happy lot. The king will come for her in a carriage drawn by six white horses."

The old spouses told him to bring his daughter to the church. Their name were Joachim and Ana. They baptized the girl and Anuszka. Her godfather presented her with a pair of scissors, and her godmother gave her a braid of gold.

As Anuszka grew older, her hair of fine gold grew longer and longer. Nobody except for her father knew where she had got the braid. When Anuszka was completely grown up and knew how to spin, she used the scissors to cut her braid and spin yarn of it. For many years, her mother would take the yarn to the queen and the old king.

Once, the young prince fell ill. No doctor seemed to be able to cure him. Somebody advised the palace people to make a cloak of the yarn so that the prince could wear it. He followed the advice. As soon as the prince put on the cloak, he recovered, though not completely.

After some time, he went for a walk to the woods. The sorceress came his way. She asked him, "Where are you going, young prince? You look ill. Would you like a healing concoction or herbs? It would cure you."

She picked some grass, heaped it, and made a fire. "Go where the smoke goes."

The prince thought, "What if the smoke heals me indeed!" He gave a gold piece to the sorceress, said thank you, and followed the smoke. The sorceress laughed behind his back, "He, he. He gave me a gold piece, but he will not be cured."

The prince followed the smoke on and on until he got out of the woods. He stopped behind a bush, seeing a girl at a spinning wheel. He stood there looking at her, and she sat there spinning. And pasturing a cow, too. It was by spinning that she had earned the money to buy the cow. Their misfortune was over; the family could afford good meals now.

The prince approached Anuszka from behind the bush. Seeing him, she got scared, took her spinning wheel, and rushed home. However, the prince found the way to her house. Anuszka hid in a safe place. He went straight to her mother and said that he wanted to see the girl with a braid of gold. Her mother replied that there was no such girl in the family. But he knew she was there. He did not hesitate to make a proposal, for he knew where the gold yarn for his healing cloak had been coming from.

The parents begged the prince to give up his intention, saying that their daughter was too poor to marry such a rich groom. But the prince held his man, and the girl's parents agreed.

The young prince arrived, and wedding preparations began. Bells were tolling, and crowds were coming. The sorceress asked around, "What is the holiday? Where are you hurrying like busy bees?" "Get off my back," everybody answered, "I have no time for chatting with you."

Dismissing her questions, people rushed to the church. A carriage was already approaching it, drawn by six white horses. Inside it, Anuszka was sitting together with the young prince.

The sorceress could not keep from playing a nasty trick on them. She ran to catch up with the carriage but tripped over a tree stub and hurt her leg. That moment, the Tom bell began to toll.

"Help! Anybody!" the sorceress screamed.

Nobody stopped to help her. A royal wedding was a sight not to be missed. I was there too, and I had on a dress of paper, boots of glass, and a hat of butter. When we were going to the church, the weather grew hot, and my hat melted. When we were walking down the cobbled street, my boots cracked. Finally, when we were returning from the church, it started to rain; my dress got wet and tore completely.

A PRESENT FOR THE KINGS' GODSON

A king had a newborn son; so he asked two neighbor kings to be his godfathers. They arrived and stayed in the castle. Their room had a window that gave into the kitchen. When the kings went for a walk, the cook happened to hear somebody talking in the room. He looked out of the window and saw the kings' guardian angels discussing what they could give to their godson as a present. One of them said, "May he grow smart as soon as he turns ten." The second one added, "May whatever he wants come true since he is six."

They baptized the little prince Wilhelm. When he had grown up a little, the cook became his friend. The prince turned six; the cook told him, "Willy, make a wish." "What kind of a wish?" "For instance, for this water to turn into wine."

The prince made a wish. The water did turn into wine. The cook grew thoughtful and finally came up with a request. "Willy," he said, "please wish a castle in the middle of the sea. We should be brought to the castle too."

They found themselves in a castle, indeed.

"Willy, make a wish for your godfather's daughter to get here."

She was there in no time. She had been staying in the castle for a couple of days when she went out to have a look at the sea, the cook grabbed her by the legs and threw into the water. She drowned. The cook and the prince were all by themselves. The cook said, "Willy, make a wish for the other godfather's daughter to get here."

She was there in no time. She had been staying in the castle for a couple of days when she went out to have a look at the sea, the cook grabbed her by the legs and threw into the water. She drowned, too.

The kings looked for their daughters desperately but never found them. The cook and the prince continued to live in the castle. After some time, the cook grew sick of it and said, "Willy, I feel bad here. Make a wish for us to come back to your father."

The prince made the wish, and they found themselves in his father's palace in no time. Nobody recognized him, for the slaves had been long replaced. The cook applied for a job. They employed him as a cook, and the prince became his kitchen hand. They served for several years. The cook developed a habit of drinking. He lost his memory and forgot that the prince was to become smart when aged ten.

As soon as the prince turned ten, he came to remember what he had done. He came to his father but did not confess to be the prince. He asked the king to give a lavish feast, saying that he had a nice surprise for the guests. "Watch out!" the king said. "If your surprise turns out to be not too nice, I will have you decapitated. The feast is going to cost me five hundred gold pieces."

The kitchen had asked him to invite his godfathers, the neighboring kings, to the feast. Invitations were sent to them; they came. The king ordered his hunters to kill some game for the feast. They brought game. The cook took his kitchen hand to an inn and drank. At about ten in the morning, the king's servants came for him, "Come home, cook," they said, "you have to prepare the meal." The cook replied, "I will not cook today. Another glass, innkeeper!"

The slaves grew sad and went home. They were afraid lest the king should dismiss them. They did not tell the king a thing and came again for the cook at noon. "You should be serving now, cook. Go to the kitchen, or else the king will dismiss us all." "I will not cook today. Another glass, innkeeper! No cooking today."

The slaves returned in despair. Water was cold and meat uncooked. It was high time they began to serve. At half past twelve, the cook said, "Let us go, Willy."

They came to the kitchen; the cook poured water into the pot.

"Willy, make a wish for it to become soup; the best soup the guests have ever tasted. Make a wish for the meat to get roasted deliciously. Pastry carp will come next. Make the wish, Willy. Let everyone who tries it lick his fingers. Now get smeared as if you had been cooking, and let us go to the guests."

They appeared in front of the guests. The king said, "So what is your nice surprise, kitchen hand? The feast has cost me five hundred gold pieces. Beware! If you fail to please the guests, I will have your head blown off!" "Your Majesty," the prince said, "I am not afraid." He fished a small box out of his pocket and came up to one of his godfathers, "Did you have a daughter?" "I did, but she is missing." "Would you like to see her again?" "If you bring her back to me, kitchen hand, I will let you marry her and give you my entire kingdom."

The prince snapped his fingers on the box and said, "I want this king's daughter to come here."

She did come. The prince took her by the hand, and they came up to the king together. He hugged his daughter and said, "Nobody will do you any harm, kitchen hand. Please go on."

The kitchen hand came up to his other godfather. "Did you have a daughter?" "I did, but she is missing." "Would you like to see her again?" "If you show her to me, kitchen hand, I will let you marry her and give you my entire kingdom."

He snapped his fingers on the box again. "I want the king's missing daughter to come."

She took her by the hand, and they came up to her father together. "Your Majesty, is this your daughter?" "She is. She shall be your wife, kitchen hand. I give you my kingdom; not one hair of yours will fall to the ground."

The kitchen hand came up to his own father. "Your Majesty, did you have a son?" "I did, but he is missing." "Would you like to see him again?" "Bring him back to me, kitchen hand, and you will have my entire kingdom."

Smeared as he was, the kitchen hand hugged the king, "I am your son!"

The feast went on. The prince told the neighboring kings, "Godfather, you have two daughters. I will marry the elder one; let the younger have your kingdom. You, Godfather, have an only daughter. She should rule your kingdom. I do not need your kingdoms, for I have mine to rule."

The matter was settled. They were going to put the cook to death, but he died of grief before they did, and demons took him to hell.

ABOUT THE KING'S SON

Once upon a time, a king wanted to start a war; but he did not have enough money. He borrowed some money from a rich sorcerer named Miloyardin and marched off. The sorcerer had a daughter; she asked her father if the king could marry her. Her father replied, "If you want to be the king's wife, come with me."

He took her to the royal palace, turned the queen into a horse, and put his daughter in her place. He made her look just like the queen.

The king had a son who went to school.

When the king returned from the war, the fake wife complained about his son. The king said, "Find a way to get rid of him."

His son was just returning home from school. He was carrying sweet buns. He went to the stables and gave the buns to the horse.

She kicked him. He said to her, "You wretch! I feed you, and you dare kick me!"

The horse replied, "Your mother will give you soup and sweets for dinner today. Do not eat anything. Tell her that you are going to eat a little later. But make sure you do not eat a morsel, for you will be poisoned. Give the food to a dog."

The prince went to his room to study. His mother brought him dinner. He said that he would eat later, claiming to be very busy. His mother left the dinner and went out of the room; he gave it all to a dog. The dog ate it and died.

On the following day, he came to the stables on his way from school again to give some sugar and buns to the horse. She kicked him. He said, "You wretch! I give you food, and again you kick me!"

She replied, "You are going to have soup, meat, and sweets for dinner today. Eat the soup and the meat and give the sweets to a dog. Tell them you have lots to learn."

The queen brought him dinner. He ate the soup and the meat and hid the sweets in his pocket. On his way to school, he threw them to a dog, and the dog died at once. The queen complained to her husband, saying that nothing would work. The king ordered his tailor to make a suit with special buttons. As soon as one pressed the buttons, he would be torn to pieces. His son came to the stables on his way from school again to give some sugar and buns to the horse. She kicked him. He said, "You wretch! I give you sweets, and again you kick me!"

She replied, "Your father ordered that a suit should be made for you. The suit will have special buttons. If you press them, you will be torn to tiny pieces. Get some money, see the tailor, and ask him to make a suit just like that. When it is ready, hide the spare suit in a chest. When your mother brings you the suit your father has ordered for you, tell her that you are too busy studying and that you will try on the present later."

He followed her advice. When his mother left, he hid the present suit in his chest, took out the spare one, and put it onto the chest. When his mother ordered him to wear the new suit, he wore his and was unhurt.

"There is no way we can get rid of our son," the king told his wife. "Give up the idea."

He went to make a round of his kingdom. The king's wife scratched her face and tore her hair. When the queen was back, she said, "Your son has beaten me so hard."

The king told his son that he was to be put to death on the next day. His son took some sugar and buns and brought them to the horse. She kicked them and said, "Ask your father to let you ride me twice around the palace before you are executed tomorrow."

On the following day, crowds gathered by the royal palace. The king's son was to be executed at midday. The prince came to see his father in the morning, begging him to let him ride his favorite horse for the last time. His father agreed. The horse jumped across the mountains and brought the prince to another king's garden. She gave her bridle to the prince and said, "Ask the gardener to give you a job. If you need something, shake the bridle."

The king's son had a special appearance—he had a star-shaped mark on his breast and golden hair. He put on simple clothes, and the gardener gave him the job of growing flowers.

Once, the king's daughters were walking in the garden. All the gardeners made bouquets; he made one and gave it to the youngest one. She took a ring off her finger, wrapped it in a handkerchief, and gave it to him.

The king's two elder daughters soon got married. Many princes proposed to the youngest one; but she would not marry them. She said she wanted to marry a gardener. Her father consented.

The king's son shook the bridle; the horse galloped up to him; he mounted her, put on a mask, and came to the palace. The king's youngest daughter was expecting him to look handsome at the wedding. Seeing him ugly, she did not want to marry him anymore. But the king forced her.

After the wedding, the neighboring princes waged war on the king to revenge his daughter's refusals. The king was losing every battle. The queen reprimanded her husband, "It is your fault! I should not have married you!" He replied, "I will go and fight, too."

He mounted a horse with his back forward, reached a field, killed the horse, and shook the bridle. The horse came galloping. He mounted her, rode to the place where the war was on, jumped off the horse, and ordered her to clear some space for him. The enemy was shattered. The soldiers lifted their hands up, begging for mercy.

The king, his wife's father, ordered his people to keep the warrior where he was so that they could find out who he was. But the horse came galloping for him, took him to the sky, and descended right where he had killed another horse. He shot a couple of crows, brought them to his wife, and said, "I am back from the battlefield."

She was angry with him and did not reply. After some time, the king marched his troops off again. His daughter told her husband, "They wage war on my father again because of you." He replied, "I will go and fight, too."

He mounted a horse with his back forward, reached a field, killed the horse, and shook the bridle. The horse came galloping. He mounted her, rode to the place where the war was on, and jumped off the horse. Having got some space cleared for him, he began to fight again. The enemy's king begged him, "For pity's sake! I will never fight anymore, and I will prohibit the next seven generations of my successors to do so!"

His father-in-law ordered his people to watch the knight closely and shoot him if he mounts a horse. They hurt his leg, and the horse fell onto the ground. He wrapped his wound with a silk kerchief, and they galloped again. He killed some crows and brought them to her wife again. Yet, she was angry with him. All of a sudden, their messenger came and said, "You are to come to a ball."

His wife agreed to come, but he would not.

The messenger came again and said, "The King wants to see you." He replied, "I have to walk as much to see the king as he has to see me."

The king came to see him to find a locked door. Peeping at the window, he saw his son's-in-law leg wrapped with a silk kerchief. The king realized him to be the unknown knight who had defeated everybody.

The king's son took off the mask, shook the bridle; and the horse arrived. She turned into the queen and said, "I am your mother."

The king, his father, came too. They sent the woman who had been pretending to be the queen away; and the king's son began to rule the two kingdoms.

HOW A SIMPLE MAN'S SON BECAME THE KING AND MARRIED A SEA GIRL

Once upon a time, there was an old childless king. He could not decide who should be his heir. Noble gentlemen despised common folks; they all were malicious and cowardly. He made up his mind to choose a simple peasant and had an order communicated around his village—those who had a dexterous, smart, and handsome son were to send him to the king.

A poor peasant lived in one of the villages. He had twelve sons, all equally handsome, well-built, and dexterous. The father sent them to the king.

The king ordered that a very wide and deep moat should be dug and filled with water. He announced, "The one who jumps across the moat and back three times will become my heir."

The oldest brother made a jump but fell into the water. So did the second one. The rest of the brothers fell into the moat, too. They youngest one was to jump.

He had a horse, a gray black-legged stallion. He jumped onto his horse's back, rode a big distance away, took run, and jumped over the moat and back. He did it three times.

The king was surprised to see the youngest brother, who hardly looked to be fourteen years old, so dexterous and savvy. He ordered him to stay in the palace and said, "I would make you my heir, for you have coped with the task. Unfortunately, you have a rough peasant-like face."

The simple man's son replied, "I cannot help it. I have to live with the face until I die."

Having said it, he mounted his horse and rode to a meadow to have fun. All of a sudden, he saw a most beautiful feather carried by the wind right at him. "I wish I could get it," the simple man's son thought. He gave his horse a spur, lifted from the saddle, and got it.

He was happy and went to the king to show him the feather. Seeing it, the king said, "I do not value horseplay. If you are dexterous enough to catch the feather, catch the bird that has lost it." "Well, I will," the simple man's son replied.

He grew thoughtful. He could not invent a way of catching the bird. So he complained to his horse, "I am in trouble. The king has ordered me to catch the bird that has lost the feather." The horse told him, "Never mind. Do what I tell you. Cut my stomach open, take all the guts out, put them into a sack, and I will take you to the meadow."

When they entered the meadow, the horse said, "Put a rope through the sack; I want it to be long. Get four poles, stick them into the ground, and place the sack over them so that everybody can see the guts. Hide inside of me and hold the rope. I will pretend to be dead. Look sharp. The bird will come and peck on the guts. When it gets into the sack, pull the rope. The bird will be yours. Then take the sack, mount me, and I will take you to the king. He will see that you are as good as your word is."

The simple man's son did what the horse told him. He caught the bird. How beautiful it was! It had opalescent colorful feathers but was very fierce—not the kind to be taken with one's bare hands.

So he brought the bird to the king. The king was very happy to have such a dexterous and smart heir. He sent invitations all around, asking people to come and admire the wonderful bird. He told the simple man's son, "You have been able to jump across the moat and catch the wonderful bird. Now invent a way to change your face." "Alright. I will."

The simple man's son went to consult his horse. She told him, "Keep the key. Look into my ear. You will find a gold box with a vial of a white concoction in it. Get plenty of milk boiled, put the concoction into the milk, and wash yourself with it. You will become so handsome that crowds will come to admire you just as they are coming to admire the bird."

The simple man's son followed her advice secretly. He boiled the milk on his own, added the concoction to it, dove into it, and became even more handsome than he could imagine. He came to see the king and said, "Does my face still look like that of a peasant?" The king replied, "What a handsome boy you have become! I was going to send you to school so that you could study, but I would rather not, for there will be no getting rid of girls. Study in the palace."

The king hired teachers for him. When the studying was over, he said, "Now find a wife to match you."

"Alright, I will."

The simple man's son went to the stables to see his devoted horse. "Tell me what to do. The king wants me to find a wife to match me." The horse replied, "I have beautiful daughters; but they live in the sea. Listen to my advice: decorate a ship richly, cover the floor with carpets; prepare most beautiful garments, mirrors, perfume, and flowers to startle my daughters. Get a quick boat for yourself. As soon as you catch one of my daughters, leave the ship at once, for it will sink in no time. Make sure you waste no time and do not look back."

The simple man's son did so. The horse was not really a horse but a sorceress. She had been looking for a young man to break the spell on her daughter and finally found one.

The simple man's son brought his most beautiful decorations to the ship, hid, and waited until he saw girls coming out of the water, entering the ship, and exclaiming with joy,

"Look, look! How wonderful! Let us put on the garments and run away. It will be great fun. Their owners will come to get dressed for a ball and see their gowns missing! Let us laugh at them!"

They got dressed quickly; but one of them could not put on her shoe. The shoe was too small for her, and she would not take any other.

The man jumped out of his hide, caught her in his arms, and jumped into the boat. He tied the girl by the leg so that she could not leap into the water and brought her home.

The king was astonished by how smart and dexterous he was. To marry a sea girl!

The simple man's son did marry her and became the king's heir. His wife and he lived happily ever after. She was grateful to him for releasing her from the sea where she lived when under the spell.

HOW THE DOG GOT THE WOLF WEAR BOOTS

Once upon a time, there were the Wolf and the Dog. The Wolf came to the Dog and said, "I am going to eat you, Dog." The Dog begged, "Do not eat me, dear Wolf! I could make you boots!" "Alright, make me a pair of boots."

The Wolf came for his boots. The Dog said, "I am going to put the boots on your feet. You will look like a rich man. But do not walk on mildew and in water, or else you will lose the boots. I will not make you another pair."

The Dog took the Wolf to the barn and told him to batter manure.

While the Wolf was battering it, the Dog kept saying, "Now you have boots. If you do not believe me, look at the peasant—his are similar. Just remember what I told you—do not walk on mildew and in water."

The Wolf followed her advice and made up his mind not to go anywhere at all. He lazed for two days and got hungry. The Wolf rummaged through the woods, drank some water from the river, and waded it to see that his boots were gone. The water had taken them.

The Wolf realized that the Dog had deceived him.

The Wolf grew angry and came to see the Dog again and ask her, "What kind of boots did you make for me? Where are they?! I will surely eat you now!" The Dog replied, "I told you not to walk on mildew and in water. You heard me tell you. Do whatever you want; I am not going to make another pair for you."

"Let us go to court," the Wolf said.

They agreed to go to court. The Wolf asked the Bear and the Boar to testify for him; the Dog invited the Cat and the Cock. They all went to court. The Wolf was leading the procession, followed by the Bear and the Boar. The Wolf said to the Bear, "Climb a tree. You, Boar, hide in the leaves and lie still until I call you. I will settle my accounts with the cheeky Dog on my own. If you see I cannot cope with her on my own, come and help me. We will tear the Dog into pieces."

The Dog walked totally unaware of the Wolf's scheming. The Cock was marching proudly behind her, followed by the Cat. The Cock was speaking to himself, "Well, well, well, well, well..."

Sitting on a tree branch, the Bear heard it and thought, "They must be conspiring to eat the Wolf."

Behind the Cock, the Cat was marching, his tail in air. Looking at him, the Bear told the wolf, "We are in trouble. He has got a pike to stab us all." The Wolf replied, "Nonsense. We can cope with them. We are strong enough. The three of us are the strongest in the forest. I could gulp all of them down all by myself." The Bear replied with a sigh, "You are right. I can kill them all with my heavy paw. They would not say a word before I tear them to shreds."

The Boar was listening under the leaves, staying silent. He wagged his tail, and the leaves made noise. The Cat heard it and thought it to be a mouse. It leaped on it and grabbed the Boar by the tail. The Boar could not understand what was happening and jumped out of his hide. The Cat was so happened that he climbed the very branch on which the Bear was sitting. The Bear got scared, too, thinking that the Cat had killed the Boar and was about to attack him. The Bear climbed higher until he climbed the top of the tree and there was no more place to go. The Cat kept climbing as if to get him.

The Bear was scared to death; he fell onto the ground and died.

The Cat sat on the tree; the Boar ran away; the Dog and the Wolf were left facing each other.

The Wolf jumped at the Dog, thinking, "If I cannot cope with her on my own, my friends will help me." Yet, there was nobody to help—the Bear was dead, and the Boar had disappeared.

The Dog was big and strong; and the Wolf had been fasting for three days and was very thin. They began to bite each other. Finally, the Dog bit the Wolf to death.

The animal court gathered to discuss the case and declared to the Dog, "You are right," and gave a certificate to the Dog to state it. The Dog hid the certificate; but mice ate it. The Dog came to hate the Cat for letting the mice eat the document. No dog has been able to keep from attacking a cat to punish it since then.

The Cat is angry with mice. Whenever he sees one, he has to eat it.

It has been this way since then: the Dog dislikes the Cat; the Cat dislikes mice, and the Wolf dislikes the Dog.

GUSTEK'S MISFORTUNE

Nobody remembers when it happened. Once upon a time, two brothers lived in a village. The elder one's name was Karol, and the younger one's name was Gustek.

The elder brother lived in a pretty brick house. He had a large household, many horses, plenty of cattle, two workers, and a servant.

Gustek lived in a clay hut and had nothing but a plot of field, which lay on a hilltop and was very stony. Gustek had a single horse, which was half-blind and could barely drag its hooves. It is no wonder that Gustek's children were always hungry. How can one feed a family of five stomachs? Gustek's household was also unfortunate—either a pig or a cow would die, or hens would stop laying eggs, for which the hungry children waited desperately every day. Everybody in the village knew how tough Gustek's lot was. If somebody was having a trouble with his household, they would say, "It must be Gustek's misfortune." Some pitied Gustek, "Poor man! He works his fingers to the bone and has nothing." Some would merely wave their hand, "We cannot help him! He is destined to be this way!"

Gustek's brother Karol, greedy and mean, pitied Gustek the least. He was always grumbling and complaining—he had a cruel and cold heart. Karol would often go to the fair in a carriage drawn by two fat horses and see Gustek dragging along. The rich brother would lift his head high, turn away, and pass by as if he could not see him. Sometimes, Gustek came to borrow something from his brother, but he never agreed. He would claim his grain to be unthreshed, his flour to be still at the mill; he would pretend to have borrowed money to someone else... Gustek gave up visiting him.

Once, Gustek was returning from the market. Passing by his father's house, he saw it all lit up. The whole village was echoing with music. Gustek remembered it to be Karol's birthday. So he forgot about his grudge and decided to call at his brother. When he entered the house, the music nearly deafened him. Longs table were standing all along the yard with pots of pork, chicken, and goose on them. Servants were fussing around the tables, carrying jugs of beer. A servant ran to tell his master about his brother's visit; but Karol would not come to see Gustek or invite him to dine; instead, he ordered the servant to take his brother to the kitchen.

Gustek felt like crying; he was about to leave, but suddenly he saw various dishes standing on the kitchen table, smelling delicious. Gustek felt awfully hungry.

All of a sudden, he saw a figure in front of him. It was as thin as a rod; its head was the size of a nut, and its legs were like straws. He could not understand if it was a human being.

"Who are you?" Gustek asked in a scared voice. "I am your misfortune," the ugly creature squeaked, "Let me chew on the bone a little, I am starving." "You see," Gustek replied, "there is nothing to eat here unless you get inside." "I will. I am so thin!" Misfortune sneaked into the bone at once. Soon, Gustek could hear her chewing noisily." Gustek thought, "How sick I am of you, disgusting monster! You have been sponging me off for years. But I know what I am to do now!"

He took a knife out of his pocket, cut a poplar branch off, made a plug, and stuck it into the bone, nailing it in with a stone. Misfortune squeaked and asked him to release her. Gustek would not listen to her. "Stay here, ugly monster!"

he said. "You have been tormenting me so long, let me have a rest."

He hurried to the fence and buried the bone under a lilac bush.

Gustek began to go up in the world. His cows began to milk better; his pigs grew rapidly, and his hens lay eggs every day. Even the half-blind horse was alive and kicking again. Little by little, Gustek climbed out of poverty. He even bought himself a couple of horses and built a house to replace his clay hut.

His elder brother grew envious. He was a wicked, merciless man, and never meant good. At last, he could not take it anymore. He went to his younger brother and began to enquire about the reason why he had become so rich. Gustek told it as it was. Listening to it, Karol thought, "I will not you be my equal, brother! I will release your Misfortune so that she can sponge you off again."

Karol said goodbye to his brother, went home, and dug the ground under the lilac bush at the fence. He got the bone and asked, "Gustek's Misfortune, are you here?" "I am, let me out, good man! Karol took the plug out of the bone. Misfortune leaped at his neck, squeezing it and squeaking, "My dear! I will stay with you till you die!"

Karol was afraid. He tried to shake Misfortune off but failed. She clung violently to him. He ran to his house and felt something on his back, strangling him, growing heavier all the time. He grew tired as if he had been working the whole day.

Hardly had Karol recovered his breath before he could go to the ploughmen in the field when he saw a shepherd shouting that his best cow had got caught in a bog. The rich man gathered people; they scarcely pulled the half dead cow out. As soon as he got home, he saw his wife running and crying that one of his three pigs had broken its leg. They had to slaughter the pig. Gustek's Misfortune was now ruling the rich man's household. His cattle seemed plagued; his horses were dying; wind was tearing off his roof; his carriages were breaking up half way to the destination.

His wealth seemed to disappear into thin air. Only the wind was roaring in his empty stove, and Misfortune was dancing in the empty lumber room, whooping and screeching. A couple of raw-boned crocks were standing in the yard. Karl, who used to be rich and greedy, was working in the nearby, as skinny as a rake.

Gustek was a nice and sensible master. He did not forget his days of poverty and helped whoever turned to him. He was admired and respected. Gustek lived to be very old. When dying, he instructed his children to be honest, cooperative, and helpful to those plagued by misfortune.

THE TWO BROTHERS

Two brothers lived in a village. One was rich, and the other was dog poor. The rich one did not mind mixing with his poor brother; but his wicked wife did. The rich brother had not crossed his poor brother's threshold in seven years.

One morning, the poor brother went to the forest with his barrow to get some firewood. His wife gave him whatever they had to eat—half a loaf and half a cheese so that he could refresh while at work. Nothing but a handful of flour was left for the hungry children. Having filled his barrow with firewood and tied it up, the man sat down to eat the meal his wife had given him.

Hardly had he started when a boy wearing a grayish shirt appeared in front of him. Approaching him, the boy said, "God bless the meal!" The poor man replied, "Please sit down and share it with me." He broke the loaf and the cheese into halves at once. The boy ate with zest and then said, "Make three wishes. You will get whatever you want for giving me food; just do not forget what is the best of all."

"Well, listen. I have a wicked, quarrelsome neighbor, and she is always doing her best to do me harm. As soon as my children enter the yard, she sends them away, shouts at them, and sometimes even fights. I would love her to live in peace with me." "She will," the boy said. "Your neighbor will come to see you tonight."

"The second thing is," the poor man said, "I have a brother, but she has not visited me for seven years, for he is angry with me. It makes me feel so sorry. I would like us to make it up." "You will," the boy said, "your brother will come to you tonight. What is the third thing?"

"Several years ago, I had everything. I lived in plenty. I have a large chest in the attic. It used to be full; but now it is empty. I would like the chest to be full of ducats." "You will have it before you come back home." Having said it, the boy disappeared.

The poor man brought his barrow home. His wife came out to get the firewood. The man said, "You must be hungry, both you and the children. I feel like eating something, too. Go to the attic, get a handful of ducats from the chest, buy some bread, buns, and meat at the inn, and cook a supper."

His wife was petrified. She could not believe her ears and was speechless. Her husband went on, "Do what I am telling you." "You must be mad! How can I get a handful of ducats from the chest? There is not a single one in it!" But the man insisted, and his wife had to go to the attic.

She glanced into the chest—it was full of ducats. Surprised, she took a handful, then another, and more, and returned to the house. She took three ducats, the eldest child, the barrow, and went to the inn.

Seeing her coming back, the neighbor's children noticed the poor woman was carrying several loaves and beer bottles, a quarter of beef, a quarter of veal, beef, and much more. They rushed inside and told everything to their mother. She wondered where the poor people had got it all and sent her children to overhear under the neighbor's windows in the dark.

The poor man's wife put the meat into the pot and put it on fire.

Her husband told her, "Go to my brother and borrow a quart so that we can count the ducats." She did. The brother's wife was dying to know why the needed the quart but failed to learn.

The poor man took to work, counting and measuring the ducats. "We have fourteen quart of ducats," the man said. "Now send a child to take the quart back." They returned the quart to the man's brother.

However, the latter was curious and studied the quart thoroughly. He saw something shiny, lifted it with a knife, and saw a ducat. The rich man shook the quart, and fourteen more gold ducats fell out of it. He could not resist asking his brother, "How did you measure whatever you measured leaving fourteen gold ducats in there? I have brought them to you!" Walek replied, "Take them, brother. I have plenty." "Where did you get them?" his brother asked. The honest Walek told him the story as it was.

The neighbor's children told their mother what they had seen in the window. The wicked neighbor would not believe it and went to visit her neighbors on her own. Walek gave them a warm welcome and gave a treat to both his brother and the neighbor.

The rich men came home and told his wife what he had heard from his brother. She said, "Maybe he agreed with demons." "Nonsense! A devil would not have given him so much money for a loaf of bread and a piece of cheese!" They racked their brains over what they could do to have as many ducats as the poor brother had.

The husband told his wife, "Listen, I am going to take some bread and cheese tomorrow and go to the place where my brother was." His wife gave him a large loaf and two cheeses. When he came to the forest, he filled his barrow with firewood, tied it up, and sat down to have a meal.

Hardly had he taken out the loaf and cheese when he saw the boy wearing a grayish shirt coming, just as his brother had told him, and saying, "God bless the meal!" The rich man replied, "Please sit down and share it with me."

The boy came up to him, and he gave him half the loaf and a cheese. They ate their lunch together, and the guest said,

"Make three wishes. You will get whatever you want for giving me food; just do not forget what is the best of all."

The rich man grew thoughtful but could not think of a wish to make. He said, "I need my wife's advice." "Alright," the boy said, "you will not even have to come back here to tell me the answer. Whatever wishes you make before sunset will come true."

The rich man came home and told his wife about his encounter with the boy. "Who knows if it is true. We should try, anyway! I want our cow to grow new horns."

She had not finished when she saw a servant running to them from the cow shed and shouting that the cow had grown nice white horns. They rushed to the cow shed and saw it to be true.

The wife said, "I wonder if the horns are well-rooted." She grabbed one of the horns and twisted it until it was left in her hand. Her husband grew angry, "It had just grown! Why did you twist it off? May the horn grow on your forehead!"

It happened at once. No matter how hard they pulled it; nothing helped. It seemed to be glued forever. The whole village had come to see what was going on; but nobody could give an advice.

The sun was about to set, so their time was running out. The man grew sad and thought aloud, "Two of my wishes have come true. There is one left until the sun sets. I have to rescue my wife." All their relatives begged him to save her. The rich man could not but agree and say, "May the horn fall off!"

The three wishes had come true, and the rich man's scheming was to no avail.

The poor man lived in plenty ever since.

MIRACLE AT THE MILL

Not far from the small town of Dombruwna, a brook was driving the wheels of a large mill. Everything was in motion there. Numerous wagons were bringing grains to the mill and taking flour to the neighboring villages.

Miller Marenski was a most thrifty man. He got up at dawn and worked tirelessly until sunset. At harvest time, he would often stay awake throughout the night, calculating the money he had to pay for milling grain, and hiding it in a heavy oak chests.

The miller was terribly greedy. Not only did he work without rest but also would not let his wife and son have an easy time, let alone his worker. They often cried, and sometimes even quarreled with him. The miller was getting richer day by day. The more silver thalers he put in his oak chests, the greedier he became.

One winter was especially cold. The Lake of Dombruwna and the brook on which Marenski's mill stood were icebound. Many homeless poor men were begging for food; they often came to rich masters. They did not pass by the miller's estate without knocking at his door. However, he would not listen to them. He never gave a piece of bread to a beggar. Instead, he sent them away, calling them useless mouths.

Once, a snowstorm began in the evening. The wind was roaring in the chimneys; windowpanes were blooming with white frost flowers. Suddenly, there was a timid knocking on the door. A traveler dusted with snow was standing at the threshold.

"What do you want?" the host murmured angrily. "Do you have a job for me?" the traveler asked. The old miller was outraged. He yelled that he had nothing to do in winter, and his worker was idling around. The traveler asked the miller to give him a place to sleep and something hot to eat, for he had been traveling long and was exhausted and hungry. The miller would not listen to him. "I have neither a free corner nor food for a stray thing like you!" he shouted and ordered the poor man to go out of the house and close the door behind him.

The traveler did so; but before he walked along the snow-covered path, he lifted his walking stick, waving it to the left and to the right, and muttered something.

Having come to the mill the next morning, the miller was petrified. Hordes of mice were sitting on sacks of flour and grans, which were standing in neat rows along the walls.

The miller clutched his head. The wealth was melting. The mice would not leave a single grain... What could he do? "Help!" he cried for his wife, son, and worker.

But what could they do? They were not afraid of people and would not run away.

The miller's timid wife said, "You are being punished for sending the poor man away!" The miller was terrified. He begged his worker, "Janek, run after the traveler I sent away yesterday. It must be him who has done it. Ask him to come back, beg him. Give him whatever he wants as long as he can send the pest away. I will give you something too, Janek. Run as swiftly as you can. He cannot have gone far away in a night."

Janek put on his coat and hat and ran. The road led straight to the village. Janek soon found the traveler in the hut of a poor man who had pitied the traveler and let him in for the night. Janek begged the traveler to come back to them. The traveler stood up, thanked the host, and went to the mill.

How happy the miller was to see him! He hugged and kissed him, apologized, promised to be thankful forever and to pay generously if only he sent the mice away.

The traveler wanted the miller to make an ice hole on the lake surface. He shook his stick to the left and to the right, struck the floor, and muttered something. Miraculously, all the mice ran up to him at once. Beating his stick, the traveler headed for the door and out. The mice followed him on the stairs, through the yard, and finally to the lake. There were hordes and hordes of them. The traveler stood at the ice-hole and stuck his stick in the cold water. The mice began jumping into the lake. All jumped, and all drowned. Not a single mouse was alive.

When the last mouse disappeared into the water, the miller ran up to the traveler. He gave him all kinds of presents and could not stop saying thank you.

It changed the greedy miller. He became kind and nice to people and never sent beggars away.

And mice never came back.

LARK AND THE WOLF

he Lark made a nest in the woods. The Mole came to ruin the nest.

The Lark was flying around, squeaking and begging the Mole not to touch his home, for his little nestlings would die.

All of a sudden, the Wolf was there. He listened to the Lark squeaking and asked, "Why are you squeaking? Are you hungry? I have been running the whole day looking for a hare or something, but I cannot find anything to eat. The sun is setting; I am nearly fainting with hunger."

The Lark replied, "It is not hunger what makes me squeak. It is that the Mole wants to ruin my nestle."

The Wolf said, "I will help you if you give me something to eat." "Alright!" the Lark agreed.

The Wolf crawled up to the nestle and lay in wait for the Mole. When the Mole showed, the Wolf caught him.

"You need not be afraid now," he told the Lark, "but remember you promised to give me something to eat."

The Lark flew to the village, and the Wolf followed him. One of the families was celebrating a wedding. The Lark sat on the windowsill and peeped in. The Wolf got on his rear legs and looked through the windowpane. Servants were serving dishes.

"I am going to fly inside. Stay by the window," the Lark said. The Lark rushed into the door and started flying around the house. The guests jumped off their seats to catch him but failed. The Lark flew to the kitchen; everybody ran after him. The Wolf jumped into the window and grabbed whatever was on the table. The Lark escaped through the chimney.

"I am so full," the Wolf said cheerfully. "It would be nice to have a drink." "Follow me!" the Lark flew off, and the Wolf followed him.

Suddenly, they saw the beer brewer bringing his beer to the wedding. The Lark flew up to him and sat on the barrel. As soon as the beer brewer reached for him, he flew off to another barrel, and then to another. The beer brewer grew angry and threw an axe at him. He hit one of his barrels and not the Lark. It shed beer onto the ground. The Wolf came up to it and drank as much as he liked.

"It was a good drink!" he said, smacking his lips. "It would be lovely to have some fun." "Follow me. I will entertain you," the Lark flew to the barnyard; and the Wolf followed him.

They saw father and son threshing grain. "Watch me!" the Lark squeaked and landed on the father's hat. "Do not move, Father!" the son shouted. "There is a bird on your head!" He wanted to wave the bird off but hit the hat. The father's legs wobbled, and he nearly fell onto the ground. The Wolf was laughing himself silly in the bushes.

Suddenly, people saw the Wolf and ran after him. He scarcely escaped.

Having reached the forest, he hid under a log. "Damn him and his fun!" he thought.

THE TALE OF THE SPELLBOUND PIKE

Once upon a time, there was a stepmother. She had a daughter of her own and a stepdaughter named Kahna.

As it often happens, she would salve her daughter and neglect her stepdaughter. Her own daughter would bully Kahna, just as her mother did.

Once, the stepmother told the orphan, "Take the baskets and go to the river. Fetch me some fish and make sure you are back before sunset. If you are late, you will regret it!"

The river was not far away from the village. The girl went to the river and cried, for she did not know how to do the fishing.

All of a sudden, a pike came up. His scales were shiny. He asked her in a human voice, "Why are you crying?" Kahna told him about her stepmother and cried on. He said, "Do not cry. Lie down and have a sleep. I will help you out, because I know you to be kind and nice to all living creatures. But do not tell anybody." Kahna lay down under a lime tree and fell asleep. When she woke up, the baskets were full of fish. The girl could not believe her eyes.

When she came up to a basket and touched it, it walked to her house on its own. It was the same with the rest of the baskets. Looking out of the window, her stepmother saw what was going on and got angry with her. She shouted, "Smart, aren't you?! Who caught the fish for you?" Kahna did not say a word.

Her stepmother invented another task for her, "Collect our linen in the baskets, go to the river, wash it clean, and dry it! Make sure you return before sunset!"

The girl brought the baskets to the river, sat down, and cried.

The same Pike showed up and asked, "Why are you crying?" Kahna told him everything and cried. He said, "Do not cry. Lie down under the lime tree and have a sleep." Kahna lay down under a lime tree and fell asleep. When she woke up, the linen was clean and dry in neat piles in the baskets.

When she touched the baskets, they walked to the house on their own.

Her stepmother was standing at the threshold. Seeing the linen clean, she simmered with anger and said, "Take the ladle with a hole in it. Go to the river and do not come back until you have ladled us full buckets of water."

What could the poor orphan do? She took the ladle and the buckets, came to the river, and cried.

Her stepmother was curious to know who had been helping Kahna. She ran out of the house and followed the girl secretly to see what was going on with her own eyes.

When the girl bent down to ladle water into the baskets, her stepmother sneaked up behind her and nearly pushed her into the river.

All of a sudden, the Pike leaped out of the water and pushed the wicked stepmother so hard that she sank.

The Pike shook off his scales and turned into a handsome prince. He married Kahna. They gave a lavish wedding feast and lived happily ever after.

OSTRUDA STONE

I am going to tell you a story as I they used to tell me when I was a child.

Near Ostruda, there is an old town called Woriny.

Many years ago, a German knight named Dietrich was its ruler. He was a famous merrymaker. He was portly and tall; he had a black beard and wore a cloak with a black cross on it, and a sword on his belt. Dietrich would come on horseback from Ostruda to his favorite inn. The innkeeper would make a low bow to him and take his horse to a stable. Frowning, Dietrich would enter the inn. Long benches and narrow tables stood along the walls. Girls would run out of the kitchen, carrying dishes, and the innkeeper would serve a silver jug of wine and a large cup to the nobleman, pour some wine into the cup, and offer the drink to him.

Once, Dietrich was reclining on a bench after a substantial meal.

The door opened, and several men came in. They made a low bow to Dietrich. They were counselors and the burghermaster who ruled the town.

"Most Illustrious Lord!" they said. "Our town is growing." "It is good news," the knight interrupted mockingly. "He, he, he. My estate is growing, too."

The men were confused. "It is, Lord. Everybody knows your estate to be the largest in the town. We were going to ask you for something." The knight gave a wave of his hand. "Gracious Lord! Many craftsmen who make all kinds of things and many merchants live in our town. But the town is small, and people are nearly suffocating. We need more space to work." "Hmm, you say people are suffocating?" the knight asked in a surprised voice, "What are people? They are like grass. When cattle graze, the grass grows even greener and taller. Why would we care about the hungry poor folks?"

The men lowered their heads. Only one of them continued to persuade the wicked knight. "Gracious Lord! Our community has agreed to ask you for a plot of land. We will pay well."

Hardly had he finished when the knight sprang up, "Go away!" Dietrich shrieked, "Now! Beggars! I will have your heads cut off and tell my people to pave the market square with them! Out!"

The man walked away sadly. "Listen, brothers," the burghermaster said when behind the door, "let us come to see him once again after he finishes the jug." Everybody agreed eagerly. They decided to come to the knight again and hope that he would relent.

For a long time, they could hear him laughing in the inn, "He, he, he! They want land! Sons of beggars! He, he, he!" Having finished the second jug, Dietrich added, "Go and suffocate, lazy things! I do not care!"

Several days passed. When the knight came to the inn again and sat at the table, the men came to him once again and asked him for some land. Dietrich grew thoughtful. He thought for a long time silently. "What if he refuses? What is he says nothing..." one of the men said in a scared whisper.

At last, the knight spoke, "Alright. There is a large stone on the border of my estate in the suburbs. Have you seen it?" "Yes, sir," the guests replied in a chorus. "So," the knight went on, if there is a man in your town to lift the stone and carry it elsewhere, I will give you as much land as the strong man can get for you. The spot where he drops the stone will be the new town border. I give you time until Saint Michael's Day. Do you understand me?" Dietrich said after a moment's silence.

"We do, sir," the burghermaster replied. Not waiting a moment, he told the secretary they had brought along to draft the agreement as quickly as he could, for the innkeeper was carrying a jug of wine again. The knight signed the agreement; the men made a bow and left.

Dietrich drank and laughed at the town dwellers…

Smith Grabosz stood at the anvil, hammering the hot iron violently. His wife was sitting at the threshold with a baby in her lap. Grabosz had thirteen children, so he always had a lot to do and was short of time. His two elder sons already helped him, but they had a lot to learn. It was about midday. The shadow of a pillar by the smithery was pointing at the house door like a huge sharp finger, as if to remind those who had been working hard it was lunch time.

Grabosz had just stopped working when the burghermaster and the counsellors appeared in his yard. "Hello!" they greeted the smith, taking their hats off." "Hello," Grabosz replied. "We have come to see you on business," the burghermaster said solemnly. "We need your help." He told the smith everything as it was. "Listen, Grabosz," he said at last, "You are a strong man; everybody knows it. Could you try and lift the stone? Could you carry it a little?" "I am not sure… I should try." "We have plenty of time. So try. Eat well; eat as much as you please—we will pay." "I find pea soup with meat to be the most delicious dish. Whenever my wife cooks me some and I have a good meal, I feel like I am growing stronger. Lime honey to polish it. Oh, I wish we could grow peas in stone, for we have no more land!"

The burghermaster took the smith by the arm, and they went to have a look at the stone.

The huge stone was lying by the road. There was no lifting it. "So you say we have time?" the smith asked. "We do, Grabosz. Plenty of time. I think you will cope with it.

We have a month left until harvest time begins, and we will have two more months after it. You can get stronger by lifting weights every day. I think you can manage it."
"Alright!"
The rumor spread around the town soon. Some believed Grabosz to be able to lift the stone; some merely shook their heads, "Nobody has ever lifted a weight like that."
The smith took along his eldest son and went to the stone at dawn. They dug the ground around the stone until it moved a little. Grabosz tried his strength every day. Soon, the smith noticed that he could lift the stone a very little bit.
After several weeks, he woke his son at night, and they went to the place together. The moon was shining in the starry sky. Grabosz bent down and put his arms around the stone. He made a huge effort and lifted the stone. Wow! The smith and his son returned home happily.
Finally, the day for which everyone in Ostruda had been waiting came. Crowds gathered to enjoy the sight. The smith stood near the stone. Several tall strong men, the burghermaster, and the counsellors stood nearby. Everybody was waiting for Dietrich. At last, they could hear a patter of hooves on the road. Dust rose into the air. Dietrich arrived.
The burghermaster turned to the smith, "Please begin!" Several men pulled chains under the stone and put them onto the smith's shoulders. Grabosz hunched. He made a step. People began to whisper; they made noise. Somebody cried with surprise; somebody laughed.
Only the knight was sitting on horseback, frowning, silent.
The smith was walking slowly, very slowly, but confidently, and moving forward bravely. He knew that the land he was walking on was promised to Ostruda... The crowd was following him silently. "How strong he is!" people whispered in astonishment. The smith did not stop. He was sweating hard; veins were swollen on his temples; he could

barely breathe. Yet, he kept carrying the stone slowly, farther and farther away from the town.

The knight was riding his horse along. He could not believe his eyes. He would have to give them the land!

Blood began to simmer in Dietrich's veins. He took out his sword and cut the chain around the stone heavily. People shrank back. It was a heavy blow. Grabosz lost his balance and fell down. The enormous stone pinned him down to the ground.

People rushed to help him, but it was to no avail. The smith had died before they lifted the stone. The stone still lies in the field near the town, with a chain mark on it to remind people about the strong smith who wanted to help his town.

LAZY GIRL

nce upon a time, there was a woman who had a daughter. Her name was Kasia.

She was pretty and healthy, but awfully lazy. She sat on the stove and would not do anything but sleep or eat until she turned twenty. She never washed her face or combed her hair, which was always tangled; so people called her Lazy Mophead.

Her mother had to do all the housework on her own; for if she had waited for Mophead to do something, their pots would had been smeared, their hut unswept, and their cow unmilked.

A good many times, her mother asked her to do something, saying, "Oh, Mophead, you have to learn to work. No king will come to propose to you; you will have to marry a peasant's son. He will order you to keep the house neat and clean and will not listen to your complaints about your arms hurting you." Mophead would not answer. She would just turn around and sleep on.

All girls of her age were long married, but nobody even looked at Mophead. A wife who can't wash a shirt or cook a dinner is no good, after all.

In the meanwhile, Mophead fell in love with a young forester, who lived in the nearby and visited them often.

One night, Mophead got up, wrapped a white sheet around her, just like a ghost, and walked to the forester's hut. "Are you sleeping?" she shouted. "No." "God and Saint

Anne told you to marry Mophead. Yes, you are to marry her!" and she vanished.

The forester was so scared that he could not go to sleep till morning. He got up at dawn and went to Mophead's house. He peeped in the window and saw her lying on the stove, her face clean, her hair combed, her cheeks rosy. She did not say a word and stared at him.

"Somehow, she is pretty," the forester thought but did not say a word and walked on.

The following night, the white woman appeared near the forester's hut again at the same time and shouted, "Are you sleeping?" "No." "God and Saint Anne told you to marry Mophead. Yes, you are to marry her! Or else I will drive you to a grave."

The forester grew even more scared. He realized that he could not help it and would have to marry the lazy girl who spent her days on the stove. In the evening, he came to their house and saw Mophead lying on the stove, but her face was clean, and her hair beautifully combed. It occurred to the forester that she was quite pretty, but he could not make up his mind to come in, because the house was full of guests, and walked on.

The following night, the white woman appeared near the forester's hut again and shouted, "Are you sleeping?" "No." "God and Saint Anne told you to marry Mophead. Yes, you are to marry her! Or else you will regret it! It is the last time I warn you."

The forester jumped off his bed and rushed out of the house; but there was nobody at the window.

He was so scared that he ran to Mophead's house in the morning to propose to her. Her mother agreed happily, only she asked him not to beat her. The forester promised not to, and they got married.

The two of them began to live together. The husband went to the forest at dawn and came back for lunch at midday.

When he entered the house on the first day, the woman was still sleeping, and their two cows were roaring in the shed, because they had nothing to eat. The forester fed the cows, milked them, and went to work. When he came back, there was no breakfast on the table, and the house was a mess. Mophead had a dirty face; her hair was uncombed. She was sleeping soundly on the stove.

At first, the man did not say a word and did the housework on his own. He washed the pots and cooked meals until he got sick of it. He asked for a job about five miles away from the village and took Mophead along. She would not do a thing in the new place and spent her days on the stove.

But her husband had an idea. He had an old hunting bag that hung over the bed. Once, as he got up in the morning, he said to the bag, "Listen! Cook me some breakfast; tidy the house, and do whatever should be done. If you do not, you will see what happens when I come home."

Mophead listened to him silently and looked stealthily to see if the bag was going to get off the hook and do the work. But the bag hang where it was. Mophead said to it laughingly, "You will catch it when he comes back from the forest!"

Her husband returned home and saw that nothing had been done. He spoke to it, "I am going to teach you a good lesson! Put the bag on your back, Mophead. I will give it a whopping for disobeying me."

Mophead laughed and waited to see what would happen. Her husband brought a stick and started beating the bag hard on Mophead's back. Mophead screamed, but he kept beating.

When leaving for work next morning, he told the bag again, "I want you to cook me a meal and tidy the house, or else I will beat you again."

As soon as he got out of the house, Mophead jumped off the stove and took to work. Having returned, her husband saw the house clean and the meal prepared and asked, "I think we need not teach the bag a lesson today, need we?" Mophead replied, "No, we need not." "Keep it this way," the husband spoke to the bag, "and I will never beat you. Have you got that?"

So it was ever on. Mophead got up every morning; and when her husband came back, everything was done. They forgot the bag, and nobody called the mistress Lazy Mophead. They called her Kasia.

After a short time, her mother was curious to see how her daughter lived and came to visit her. She was amazed to see her house and shed neat and clean! She was happy to know Lazy Mophead to have turned into a house-proud woman.

Her mother asked her, "How come your house is so tidy and you are so hard-working, daughter? You would not do anything when at home. Did he beat you hard?" "He did not," her daughter replied, "we beat a bag just once and did not have to do it again."

Her mother was glad to hear that. Kasia gave her a strange look and said in a shy voice, "Go outside, Mom, and bring a couple of fire logs, for one cannot get one's food for free in this house."

THE DWARF AND THE BEAR

It was ages ago, when miracles used to happen in the world. An old windmill stood at the Nida River.

In autumn, peasants would bring full bags of grain to the mill, and the miller named Smolka would mill it to flour, of which housewives made loaves and flatbread.

The miller was a kind and honest man; he did not ask much for milling; so people admired and respected him.

Everything would be fine but for one problem—an evil black dwarf had lived in the mill from olden times.

Few saw him; but he did a lot of harm. The miller did know where the Dwarf came from.

Back when the miller's late grandfather ran the mill, he employed his neighbor's son Antek to help him. Antek was very lazy. He would often feel too lazy to wash his face, so he would walk around with his face dirty and his hair uncombed. One could not make him set to work—he would run away to the garden or to the field, lie down onto the grass, and sleep. When it came to eating, Antek was number one—he ate enough for three.

He would often sneak into the lumber room to steal honey, cheese, and cream. At first, the old couple thought there were mice in the lumber room. They put a mousetrap with some lard in it—not a single mouse was caught. It occurred to the old miller that it must be Antek who had been stealing things from the lumber room. He fol-

lowed him but always failed to catch him red-handed.
At last, he managed to catch him. The old mistress made fresh cheese and took it to the lumber room. Her husband came in and hid the mousetrap under the cheese. The artful Antek was unaware of it. When everybody went to the field to harvest after lunch, Antek suddenly felt thirsty. He ran to the house; yet it was not the well what attracted him but the lumber room, where the fresh cheese stood. Antek put his fingers into the bowl; suddenly the trap caught his hand with a click. It hurt a lot. Antek shrieked at the top of his lungs with pain and fear and rushed out. The old miller heard him scream and ran into the yard, too. "You thief! At last I caught you!" he shouted, grabbing Antek by the collar.

He released Antek's trapped hand, gave him a piece of his mind, and ordered him to never steal again. Antek got obsessed with revenge.

One evening, he encountered a disgusting dwarf by the mill. His head looked like a cooking pot; his eyes reminded of a toad; he had a huge mouth and cauliflower ears. It occurred to Antek that the ugly dwarf could be a good use to him. He agreed to let the dwarf into the mill if he played nasty tricks on the old miller and caused losses to him.

The Dwarf lived in the warm dry attic right under the roof. He was too small for the old miller to see him. The sly creature slept during the daytime, hiding in the corner, and played pranks at night. He did so when Smolka's grandfather and father were alive; he kept doing so now that Smolka was the miller. He caused a lot of trouble. The Dwarf kept everyone busy at night. He would cling to the sails of the windmill and make them turn fast as if it was very windy; he would tear bags of grain and flour open; he would sneak up to the house windows and squeak like a rat; sometimes he would climb a tree and groan like an owl. When the miller and his wife were sleeping, the Dwarf would sneak into the mud room through a mouse hole, kick over water buckets, bang at the wall, make noise with the kitchen poker, jump onto the stove, and hit a pot with a pan to make even more noise. Sometimes he got into a cupboard and ruined cups and pots.

The Dwarf had even gnawed the bed legs through, and the sleepy miller and his wife fell onto the floor.

Whatever Smolka did, nothing worked. He could not even sell the mill, for everybody in the village knew who played the pranks at night.

Once autumn night, August Smolka was sitting in his house by the stove, relaxing after work. He had lit his pipe and was enjoying it—pow pow pow. He felt anxious because of the approaching night—autumn was the time the Dwarf was more mischievous than ever.

All of a sudden, there was a knock at the door, and a stranger stood at the threshold, "Hello!" he greeted him. "Hello. What is it?" "Could you let me in for the night and give me something to eat? There is no house in the nearby. I knocked at your door because I had seen light through the window."

The Miller asked the guest in but startled back—a huge black bear entered the mud room following the guest. "Come in, but leave the black monster outside!" the scared miller shouted. The man reassured him, "You need not be afraid. He is my friend. He will not do you any harm. I beg you, let us both in. The night is cold. The bear will be cold outside, even though he is furry. He would rouse all dogs in the nearby. I will take him to the mill. He will be warm and comfortable there." As if he understood they were talking about him, the bear stretched his fore paws to the miller and roared softly. The miller smiled, "Alright," he agreed, "something is wrong with the mill, though. I am afraid lest it harm your bear..." The man shook his head. "My bear has no fear. He can manage it."

The miller looked at the bear. He liked the furry guest. He went to the lumber room and fetched a bowl full of milk and a little honey on a plate. The bear licked the plate clean, licked the milk out, and nearly purred with satisfaction. Having finished the meal, he got onto his rear legs and began to dance, reeling in a funny manner, as if to say thank you for the treat. The miller and his guest sat at the table and laughed happily.

 Soon, they took the bear to the mill and strained their ears to know if the Dwarf was playing his tricks. The mill was strangely silent. Sometimes the miller could hear somebody roar fiercely and another creature squeak with fear. He was afraid to get up and see what was going on.

When the guest woke up in the morning, there was nobody in the house. He got dressed hurriedly and went to the kitchen. "Did you sleep well?" the miller's wife asked him. "Yes, I did. What about you?" "I slept badly. We were waiting for the naughty creature to start playing pranks, but he did not come. It is strange; something must have happened to him. Something weird was happening in the mill—something way roaring; something was squeaking; but we did not dare go and have a look." The miller entered the kitchen and greeted his guest, "Have you been to the mill yet?" he asked. "No, I was waiting for you. Let us go together."

They went to the mill and found the bear safe and sound. Seeing his owner, he produced a happy mutter. The guest patted him on his furry head. "You see," he said, "I guess the naughty creature was going to get out of the mill to play another trick on you. The bear saw him and started to chase him. That is why you hear him squeaking. The Dwarf must have run away and hidden in his hole."

The Miller shook his head merrily, "How nice of your bear to tame the rascal! I should give him more honey and milk."

After a substantial breakfast, the guest took his bear by the chain and walked to the gate. He thanked the milled for his warm welcome. "My pleasure! My pleasure!" the miller waved his hand. Be sure to call at me when you happen to be here again." "I will. Thank you! Take care!"

The miller lay awake at night, waiting for the Dwarf to

begin playing pranks in his house again. But he could not hear a thing. The mill was silent, too. Bags of grain and flour stood along the wall, perfectly intact. Nobody was wheeling the sails of the windmill.

Several nights passed that way. One evening, when the miller was basking by the fire, the door opened, and a disgusting flap-eared head popped into the split. It asked in a squeaky voice, "Tell me, miller, is your large black cat alive?" The Miller knew the Dwarf meant the bear at once, "Of course he is!" he replied cunningly. "He has seven kittens." "My oh my! Seven kittens!" the Dwarf screamed in a scared voice and rushed away. Nobody has seen him ever since.

NOBLEMAN AND MICHAL

A long, long time, about two hundred years ago, a man named Michal lived in a village. He was a short man but was very strong—he could lift a sack of grain with one hand as if it was a small bag and even put it on his shoulders. Michal's house stood on a forest glade; he had a small field plot and as many as fifteen children, so he had to work all day long. He had nothing but two amazingly beautiful gray horses. Everybody in the village was envious of the splendid horses.

They wanted to know what Michal gave them to eat, for it was not unusual for him and his wife to be hungry. Hearing his neighbors talk, Michal would only smile.

When he did not have enough hay for his horses, he took a scythe and a cloth and went to the woods in the evening to fetch some grass. He would bring a cloth full of grass, give it to the horses, and speak to them, "You work for me more than anyone! Of course, I need to take care of you. You carry all kinds of things. Eat well!"

Once in spring, Michal went to his land plot to plough the soil. He ploughed and ploughed, shouting at his horses every once in a while to make them go faster.

A German count, who was living in his estate in the nearby, happened to be traveling in his carriage along the road. He had noticed Michal's beautiful horses and set his greedy eyes on them long before. He had asked him to sell them, but Michal would not listen. So the count made up his mind to take the horses by force.

Seeing Michal ploughing his strip of land, he ordered his coachman to stop the carriage. He got out and walked across the field.

Having noticed the count, Michal hurried to the far end of the field. He stopped his gray horses and began adjusting the harness. The count ground his teeth with anger, but he could not help it and had to walk across the field.

"Hello, Michal" "Good afternoon, Your Lordship Count." The count gave Michal a pat on the shoulder. "Listen, Michal. I want to buy your horses." Michal frowned, "I will not sell them!" "I will pay well." Michal saw that there was no getting rid of the count and said, "Could you bet, Your Lordship?" "Agreed!" the count exclaimed gladly. "The horses shall belong to the one who tells better lies. If you lose, Your Lordship, you shall give me a hundred thalers. If I lose, I will give you my gray horses." "I will surely tell better lies!" the count shouted, "mark my words, you old fool! But everybody should tell lies at least three times." Michal nodded.

"I have a special cow," the count began, "I give it a concoction every day which only I know. She yields a hundred liters milk at a time." "Listen to the story that happened to me last year!" Michal replied. "Everything went topsy-turvy in this field near the woods. Crops grew in the ground, as huge as beetroots, roots up in the air. Turnips the size of a human head ripened over the ground with their tops down."

"This time you win. I lose," the count said with a grimace. "Speak on, Your Lordship Count. We shall start again and see who wins."

"Long ago, a tall pine tree grew in my garden," the count began. "It was so tall that one could see its top at a distance of a hundred kilometers. It was too thick for a hundred men to embrace it. When the pine was cut and bucked, a large village was billed, and the chippings were used to fire the stove in the estate all year long. Your hut, Michal, was also built from the logs made of that pine..." Michal did not tell much the second time. "I would like to tell you how I hunted for hares last week if you do not get angry with me, Your Lordship. Whenever I came across a hare, I poured some salt on its tail, and it was sure to come into my arms."

"Aha! I win!" the count exclaimed joyfully." "Right. Now tell your third portion of lies."

"I will tell you another hunting story. Once, I had a gun with a crooked fore-end. So I took the gun and went deer hunting. Standing at the fringe of the forest, I waited. Suddenly, a deer appeared running out of the house. I could not believe my eyes—its antlers were like oak branches. At a closer look, I saw another deer near a hill behind that one; it was even better. I pointed my gun at it and shot. What do you think? I killed both deer with a single shot—the one who appeared first and the one near a hill. My gun with a crooked fore-end helped me."

Michal smiled and said nothing. He sat down on the trail of his plough, took a snuff from his tobacco box, sneezed several times so hard that the forest echoed his sneezing, and finally spoke, "So it is my turn, Your Lordship... Alright... Once, a count lived near our village. He was very fierce. When a loaf was missing in his kitchen, he ordered his people to whip all the servants and to search every house in the village for the loaf. The count had hordes of bees and too many hives to count. My father took care of the hives. The count was very tight-fisted. He counted his bees every day but always failed and had to start again. Once, the bee queen of the biggest hive, which yielded plenty of honey every year, was missing. Nobody knows why it disappeared, but the bees stopped making honey and began to disappear one by one. The count gathered the whole village and searched in everybody's pockets, thinking that somebody might have hidden the queen. Yet, nobody had a bee. The count made up his mind to go and search for it. No matter how hard he tried, he could not find it. It suddenly dawned on him the boy who had once helped him find the missing queen of another hive lived in the village. The boy was me, Your Lordship. The count came to my house, and we began to look for the bee together. At first, we climbed to heaven. It looked very beautiful.

Men and women were sitting there at tables, and angels were their company. Everybody was eating and drinking honey milk. My master was very upset to see not a single count among them. Then, we went to hell to find the bee queen. I was coming first; the count was walking behind me. Having entered the gate, we stopped at a corner to look around. What do you think we saw? The hell was full of counts. They all were boiling in tar. There were several poor peasants, too. But they were laying fire wood under the tar pots. All of a sudden, my master saw his father in one of the pots. He grew white in the face and flung up his heels. He was afraid lest his father should recognize him and pull him into the tar pot..."

"You liar!" the count shouted angrily, "How dare you talk such nonsense to me!"

He suddenly collected his wits. Obviously, Michal was the winner. The count frowned, shoved a hundred thalers into Michal's hand, and walked away without even looking at the horses.

Michal smiled and continued to plough the field.

PUNISHED FOR GUILE

Once upon a time, a wealthy landowner from a town near Olsztyn was hunting all alone in a forest that spread very far.

On a glide in the forest, there was a trap pit to catch wolves. Walking across the glide, the landowner fell into the pit.

How scared he was to see who was in there! There were a bear, an enormous snake, and a cat. Each was staring at the others with terror. The landowner flattened himself against the wall, too, and cried out for help.

He cried and cried for three days to no avail. On day four, his worker named Michal came to the forest to cut wood and heard his voice coming from the pit. He came closer to the pit and asked, "Who is there?" He could not look into the pit, because it was covered with brushwood and, to tell the truth, he was very scared. The landowner recognized the worker by his voice, "It is me, your master!" he shouted, "I have fallen into the wolf pit. Help me out. Believe me, I will pay you well."

Michal found a long stick and put it into the pit. He felt someone grasp at it. Michal pulled hard and scarcely drew the stick out. What do you think he saw? It was not his master but a huge furry bear that rushed into the woods.

Poor Michal quivered with fear, thinking that the devil had called him and then turned into a bear. Michal was going to run away when he heard the voice coming from the pit again, "Do not leave me, Michal, dear! Have a heart! I know you want to get married. I will throw a lavish wedding feast for you, just help me out."

Hearing it, Michal smiled. Even though he did not believe it to be his master, he decided to try again. He pushed the stick carefully into the pit and felt somebody climbing it at once. Michal pulled the stick, and the master seemed to be surprisingly light. Suddenly, the cat leaped out of the pit and disappeared into the woods with a meow.

"Oh dear! It must have been the devil. The pit must be full of demons." He was about to run away when his master started begging and lamenting, "Don't leave me, Michal, dear! Night is coming. I will die of fear, hunger, and cold. I will give you a household and plenty of money if you rescue me."

Michal stuck the stick into the pit again. But this time, the snake dropped off the stick with a hiss and vanished in the grass. "I can hear a human being speaking, but wild animals keep coming out of the pit!" Michal thought with surprise.

He threw the stick onto the ground; but his master begged and shouted so wildly that he could not but pity him. "Mercy! Mercy! Put your stick in here! There is nobody left in the pit but me. I will give you my estate and all the money I have if you save my life." "If he is really my master and I rescue him, he will be grateful to me for the rest of his life," Michal thought. "Even if he does not give me his estate, he will surely give me a neat amount of money."

Michal nearly ran out of steam, for the landowner was fat and heavy. As soon as he stepped on the firm ground, he yelled, "You fool! Why did you linger so long? I could have died of hunger because of you."

Michal was scared to death. He took out of his pocket a rye bread crust, which he had taken for supper, and gave it to the landowner. Having refreshed himself, the landowner leaned heavily on Michal's shoulder and walked slowly to his estate.

Having reached the threshold, he told Michal, "I do not need you anymore. You may be free."

The following morning, the worker came to the landowner. "I hope he will give me some money for the wedding," he thought. Having entered the yard, he spoke to the servants. "What do you want of him?" the servants asked. Michal told them how he had helped his master out of a wolf pit. The servants laughed and swore at him.

Many of them thought, "If I were the one who found him, I would have left him down in the pit. Let wolves eat him." The landowner was wicked and unkind.

Finally, a servant went to him and said, "Most Illustrious Master, there is the man who pulled you out of the pit yesterday. He wants to tell you something." "What?!" the landowner yelled angrily. "Who pulled me out of a pit? It is not true!" He ran out, called Michal bad names, accused him of telling lies, took a whip, and sent him away. To crown it all, he sent hounds after him. He was not too grateful, after all.

Upset and indignant, Michal returned to his hut in the forest.

Surprisingly, his door was open. He looked inside and saw the bear and the cat he had rescued lying on the floor. The snake had made itself comfortable on the stove. The three of them were waiting for him.

Michal was petrified to see the band; but the bear came up to him politely and took him to the lumber room. There was a deer, which the bear had killed for Michal. "How wonderful! I have something to roast for the wedding!" Michal flung his hands up. "Thanks a lot. "

"The cat ran up and, fawning on Michal, took him to the mud room, where a bouquet of amazing flowers was lying. "I have a wedding decoration!" Michal exclaimed joyfully. "Thank you."

At last, the snake slithered up to him, holding a gemstone that shone splendidly in its mouth. "Oh, it must be so expensive!" Michal said in a surprised voice.

He thanked the animals politely and treated them to some food; they returned to the woods.

Michal sat down onto a bench and held the gemstone. He did not know what to do with it. In the morning, he came to the landowner's estate. He was going to sell the gemstone to his master's wife, who liked gold and fancy things a lot.

When he showed the gemstone to the landowner, the latter shrieked, "You wretch! Where did you steal it? It is worth a small fortune." "I did not, Master. The snake that was in the pit with you brought it to me." "Liar! You must have killed a traveler and taken the treasure from him!"

The landowner took the gemstone from Michal and ordered his people to put him to prison. He also sent a servant of his to town to file a lawsuit at the court. They brought Michal for a trial. He told how he had pulled the landowner out of the pit. But his master swore his worker to be lying.

Having listened to the landowner, the judge spoke to Michal, "Aha, dear! Who would believe you? Do you happen to have any witnesses?" "I do!" Michal exclaimed. "There are the bear, the cat, and the snake; but they are in the forest. Call them, and they will tell you." "Nobody is going believe your nonsense!" the judge said angrily.

He was about to declare the sentence when there was a roaring sound behind the door. The door was opened, and the bear entered the hall. The cat was sitting on his back, and the snake was coiling around his neck and looking around with its intelligent eyes. Everybody was terrified; the landowner grew white and hid behind the desk.

The bear and his friends approached him. As soon as they came closer, the landowner shrieked, "Go away! Go away! I will tell the truth. The man is not guilty. It was as he said. I will pay him; I will give him everything!"

They set Michal free immediately.

The rumor about what had happened to him spread around the village. People laughed at the landowner and ridiculed him so hard that he soon ran away across the sea.

Everybody praised and respected Michal. Soon, he was appointed forester. He lived in unity with all people; then he married his bride. It was a lavish wedding feast with plenty of food and drinks. The bear, the cat, and the snake came, too. They were treated to their favorite foods—there was honey for the bear, good fat meat for the cat, and plenty of sweet milk for the snake. It was the best wedding in the village and in Poland ever.

MISFORTUNE

Once upon a time, there were two neighbors.

A neighbor's name was Kukolka, and the other's was Kukolochka.

Kukolka was very rich, and Kukolochka was very poor. Misfortune lived on his stove. It looked very much like an owl. Whatever he earned, she would either gulp or take to the rich man.

Kukolochka grew angry, for Misfortune had taken away everything, and he did not have a bread crumb in his house. He took along his wife, a jointer, and a piece of a wooden board, and went to the woods. Seeing it, Misfortune cried after them, "Hey, where are you going?" "We are sick and tired of misfortune; we are going to the woods."

Misfortune laughed and said that she was going to arrive before they reached the forest. They reached a small river, put the board across it, crossed the river, and took the board off. Looking back, they saw Misfortune running after them, carrying a log on her shoulders. She reached the bank, threw the log across the river, crossed it, and caught up with them in the woods.

Misfortune saw Kukolochka making wood wedges. She asked, "Why are you making wedges?" Kukolochka replied, "Can you see the hollow fir tree? I will hide from you in the hollow and batten the hole, for I am sick of living with you." Misfortune laughed, "He, he. I will be the first to get into the fir tree and wait for you."

She was in the hollow in no time. Kukolochka grabbed a board, shut the hole, and nailed it down with the wedges. He and his wife returned to the house, leaving Misfortune in the hollow. They chanced to find a bag of money on their way and lived in abundance ever after. Kukolochka would come to the forest every once in a while, look at the hollow, and plug the wedges deeper to prevent Misfortune from escaping.

Seeing it, Kukolka thought that his neighbor was hiding treasures in the fir tree. He came there and took the wedges out. Misfortune jumped out of the hollow and moved to Kukolka's house.

Kukolochka was now rich, and Kukolka became poor.

THE RAM BROTHER AND THE DUCK SISTER

Once upon a time, there were two children, Jas and Marysia. When their mother died; their father married again; their stepmother abused the children, reprimanded them, kept them hungry, and wanted to get rid of them. It upset their father greatly; it occurred to him that it might be better to take the children to the forest. They could encounter somebody who would take better care of them than their stepmother did. He did what he thought.

Once, the father told his children, "Get packed, children. We are going to the forest. I will be felling a tree. You will be collecting the chippings and helping me."

The father took an axe and a saw, made himself a large stick, and off they went. The father took his children deep into the woods, ordered them to sit down on a tree stub, gave them a little rye bread and butter, and said, "Sit here. You have bread to eat, so do not get bored and wait for me. I will go a little deeper into the words to fell a tree. I will call you when I finish. You will come and collect the chippings."

Having said so, he left. Soon, the children heard a smashing noise in the woods, as if somebody was felling a tree. They thought it to be their father and sat waiting for him to call them. They waited and waited; an hour passed, then another; nobody was there to be seen. Marysia grew scared and told Jas, "You know what, Jas? I am scared." "Do not be scared. Let us go and look for Daddy."

They stood up and went to the place where the smashing noise had been coming from. Having reached the tree, they saw it was the stick their father had brought from home hitting the branches. Nobody was there. "We are in trouble, Marysia. We will have to sleep in the forest. Daddy has left us and forgotten about us." Marysia began to cry, and Jas tried to comfort her, "Do not be afraid, Marysia. The moon is shining. We can see the path. Let us walk on; nothing will happen."

They walked on. They spent the whole night wandering in the woods, and nothing happened to them. None of them even tripped on a stone.

At dawn, they came out of the woods to a field. "You know, Marysia," Jas said, "I am so hungry!" "What can I give you? I have nothing," his sister replied. They walked on until they reached a small fish pond.

"You know, Marysia, I am thirsty," Jas said again. His sister replied, "Look, can you see the ram horn in the water? Get some water into it and drink it." Jas took the horn and drank water from it; and he turned into a ram, for the horn was spellbound. Seeing it, Marysia began to cry, because she was afraid of the Ram. He said to her, "Do not be afraid, sister. I will stay with you forever, and nothing will happen to you."

Marysia was not afraid anymore, and the two of them walked on. They came to a meadow, where a hay pile was standing. They were very tired and hid in the hay, lay down, and went to sleep. They slept the whole day and the whole night and woke up to see the sun high in the sky.

A landowner happened to be passing by, for the meadow lay by the road. He ordered his coachman to stop the carriage and see what was over there. The coachman looked at the hay from above, turned back, and said, "Nothing. What could be there?" But the landowner's dog kept barking; he went to see on his own, and, straining his eyes, found the girl and the Ram. He asked her who she was, where she came from, and what she was doing there. Marysia replied, "Daddy took us to the woods and left us, because our stepmother beat us hard at home."

The landowner liked the girl so greatly that he brought her to his estate, for she was pretty, sweet, and clever. She lived in the landowner's estate. When she grew up, he wanted to marry her. She refused, "Master, I am a poor girl; you found me in a hay pile. Cannot you find a better wife?"

The landowner did not care; so he married Marysia. After a while, they had a baby boy. The landowner had a cook who had a daughter Marysia's age. The cook wanted the landowner to marry her daughter; she was jealous of her young mistress. The cook was a sorceress; she knew how to achieve what she wanted.

Once, Marysia fell ill; the cook came to see her and pricked her ear with a hairpin; the mistress turned into a duck at once and flew to the pond. The sorceress put her daughter into the bed instead of Marysia and made her look just like the mistress.

When the landowner came, he noticed that his wife still had Marysia's face, but whenever she smiled or said something, she did it differently. Something must have happened; but he could not tell what. He did not tell anybody.

The Ram, who used to stick to his sister, sat by the cradle and played with the child. Once, the landowner saw the Ram lifting the baby with his horns and carrying him to the pond. He was not very surprised, for the Ram used to do so before.

In the meanwhile, the Ram came to the pond and called out, "Marysia, Marysia, dear, come out, for your baby is crying!" The duck appeared from the water, turned into a woman, and nursed the baby; then she entered the pond again and turned into a duck. The Ram brought the baby back as if nothing had happened.

When the landowner asked him where he had been, he said that he had taken the baby to a poplar three, because it gave shadow and smelled sweet. The landowner did not speak. The sorceress noticed that the landowner was beginning to understand everything. She had been hoping that nobody would learn and she would get away with that.

The Ram kept bringing the baby to the pond every day, and the mother nursed his son every day. At last, the landowner was curious to know why the Ram would take the baby to the water all the time. Something had to be wrong! He hid behind a tree near the pond and saw the mother come to her son, turn back into a duck, and enter the pond. At first, the landowner did not know what to do.

Finally, he ordered his people to slaughter an ox and to skin him. On the following day, he put on the skin and pretended to be grazing near the pond, watching and waiting. The Ram brought the baby again and cried out, "Marysia, Marysia, dear, come out, for your baby is crying!" The duck appeared from under the water, turned into a woman, and took the baby in her arms. The landowner threw off the skin, jumped up to Marysia, and pulled the pin out of her ear. They came home together. Marysia told him about the cook and her misfortune. The landowner ordered his people to punish the sorceress and her daughter, and he lived with his wife happily ever after. The Ram stayed with them.

THE SHEPHERD

A rich shepherd employed a shepherd boy to help him. The boy could play the pipe beautifully. He would lie down and play while grazing the sheep, and his dogs would drive the sheep back from the woods lest woods eat them.

Once, the boy noticed one of the ewes to differ from the rest. She was always in advance of the flock and held her head high; the other sheep strangely obeyed her. She would often stand at a distance and listen to him playing, as if she were a sentient being.

The shepherd boy came to love the ewe and tended her with great care. One late afternoon, before dewfall, the boy drove the flock, and the shepherd divided the sheep—to slaughter, for sale, and to graze. Examining the sheep, he told the boy, "Hedge the grazing sheep with fishing line; tar those to be slaughtered on the back, and those for sale on the front."

The boy saw the shepherd select his favorite ewe for slaughter. He said, "This ewe has nice fleece, Master, we should not slaughter her!" But the shepherd replied, "Nonsense! She is as good as those over there. Do what I tell you."

The shepherd boy had to drive the ewe to those to be slaughtered. When doing so, he thought, "Let him have it his way so far. I do not want them to slaughter her, though. I will claim it to be missing when I drive the flock tomorrow."

He knew an empty, half-ruined chapel to stand at the foot or a rock. He drove the flock out and hid the ewe in the chapel on the next day. He brought stones to the threshold and battened the door lest wolves come in, left some hay for the ewe to eat, and left.

After several days, the shepherd noticed that something was wrong and asked the boy, "Where is one of the slaughter sheep?" The shepherd boy replied, "I have no idea where she is, Master. Maybe a wolf has eaten her." "So you let wolves eat my sheep, you lazybones?" He began beating the boy. "You are being unkind to me. Goodbye!" Having said so, he ran away.

Walking along the road, he thought, "I am in trouble. I should take the ewe and travel far away to a place where nobody knows me, because the rumor of me being a thief will travel fast." When he came to the chapel, the ewe was not there. "A wolf must have eaten her," the boy said to himself. "She could not escape death, and I have messed everything up and lost my job. Well, there is no bringing back what is gone."

He walked on to another country and came to look at the sea. Standing on the shore, he thought, "I should board a ship and go with it; I could make a living somehow." He did. Merchants let him board the ship, and he traveled with them.

One night, something roared terribly. People cried, "Help!" and the storm whirled the ship and threw it at the rocks. It broke into small pieces. People fell into the water; so did the boy. He was about to drown and was thinking, "Am I dead or alive?"

All of a sudden, a large fish approached him and said, "You will not die, for you have rescued others!" It took him on its back and swam for a long time until they reached an island. The fish said, "Here we are. Come out onto the shore and do not be afraid, for it is the island of happiness." It added, "When you step onto the ground, you will see a stone and a bush near it. You should use the bush to make a pipe. As soon as you begin playing, your ewe will be there, and all the shepherd's sheep will come running, for she is their queen, and you rescued her from death." The fish disappeared into the sea with a splash, leaving the boy on the shore.

"Well," he thought, "what do I have to cut a pipe with? I cannot see a single hut to borrow a knife in." Suddenly, he saw another fish approaching him in the water with a knife in its mouth. He took it from the fish and quickly cut a pipe from the bush, which smelled of mahogany. When the pipe was ready, the boy hid it in his pocket, because he felt like eating rather than playing. He walked around the isle and saw it to be a beautiful place—pure sugar, delicious oranges, and cinnamon grew on trees. He ate and drank spring water, which was as good as wine, as much as he liked, smacked himself of the belly, and said, "At last, I can play. Let us see what comes."

He found himself in a most beautiful green valley. Looking around, he saw sheep grazing. and what sheep! They had fleece of silver that shone in the sun and pearl eyes; the biggest of them had fleece of gold and eyes of diamonds.

The golden ewe took off her fleece as if it was a cloak, covered the boy with it, and, miraculously, the sheep turned into a most beautiful princess. She spoke to the boy, "You saved me from the wicked sorcerer, the shepherd, who turned me into a sheep with a magic potion. I will give you all of my treasures and my entire kingdom, and you shall be my husband. Come here, girls, take off your fleece!" she cried out to the ewes.

As soon as they put their silver fleece at the boy's feet, each of them turned into a girl—the princess's maid. The boy felt so happy that he could not resist playing the pipe again. He saw a palace in the valley, and they all went there.

The shepherd boy married the princess he had obtained on his own. They lived happily on the happy isle and ruled it ever after. Nobody stood in their way, for it was far across the sea, and sea fish guarded the kingdom like an army.

ABOUT TWO GIRLS, A KIND ONE AND A WICKED ONE

Once upon a time, there was a girl who had a rough living with her family. Her stepmother was always nagging at her; the stepmother's own daughter dressed prettily and lived in abundance, but the stepdaughter was poor and often had nothing to eat.

Once, the girl went to the woods to pick berries and got lost. She wandered and wandered until darkness began to fall, but she could not find the way. The girl began to cry.

Suddenly, a woman was coming her way and asked, "Why are you crying, girl? You will not be able to find the way. Would you mind becoming my servant?" "Why not. I would love to, if you please."

The woman asked the girl to follow her. They walked on and on until they came to a big river. She spoke to the girl, "Carry me across the water." "I would love to, but I am not sure if I am strong enough." "Of course you are." The girl lifted her and carried her across the water. She was as light as a feather—the girl walked on water and did not sink. They waded the river and came to the woman's house. There was nobody inside but for two little dogs and two cats.

The woman ordered her to cook something to eat. She gave her a pea and a single grain of barley. The girl did what she was told without objecting. She put the pea and the barley grain into boiling water and saw them turn into a bowl full of porridge.

The woman said, "You will not have a lot of work. You are to cook meals, clean the pots, comb the dogs' and cats' hair, and feed them." The girl was very nice to the dogs and the cats. She took good care of them and tried to please everyone. Whenever the woman said, "Go shut the window, Cat," she did it herself for the cat or for the dog.

The girl stayed with the woman for a year. When a year had passed, the woman told her, "You have been loyal to me. Now go home. Take whatever you want for your work." The cats and the dogs told her to take the shabbiest chest from the lumber room, and she asked if she could have it. The woman gave her the chest, saying, "The chest is heavy, and you will have to walk a long way home. You do not even know the way. So harness the dogs and the cats; they will take you there." The dogs and the cats drew the chest, repeating, "Hole on hole, a chest of gold!"

Finally, they reached her house. Seeing the strange carriage and the shabby chest, her stepmother burst out laughing, "Look what a dingy chest the girl has earned!"

They opened the chest and saw plenty of gold and other treasures.

The stepmother and her daughter envied the girl's riches badly. Once, the stepmother told her daughter to take a jug and go picking berries in the woods, crying noisily. Her daughter went to the forest. She wandered in the woods and cried until the same woman came her way and asked, "Why are you crying, girl? You will not be able to find the way. Would you mind becoming my servant?" "Why, I don't."

They walked on together until they reached a river. "Carry me across the water," the woman said. "I will not; you are heavy. I am afraid lest I sink!" They waded the river on foot. The woman's feet remained dry, and the girl began to drown. The woman stretched a stick to her and pulled her out of the water.

When they reached the woman's house, she asked the girl to cook something to eat. She gave her a pea and a single pot barley grain. The girl refused to cook, saying it was too little, "What can I cook from it? It is not enough for a cat's meal!" The woman gave her more grains. When the girl began cooking, the pots grew so full that the porridge flew off until it reached the ceiling.

Once, the woman ordered her dog to close the window. The dog asked the girl to do it for him. She said, "The one who was asked should do the job!"

She was always that way. The dogs and the cats grew thin and weak.

At last, a year passed. The woman said, "You have been serving me for a year. Now it is time you returned home. What would you like to get for your work?" The girl said she wanted a chest, and it had to be the very best chest. "Alright. But it is too heavy for you. Harness the cats and the dogs; they will carry it for you."

The girl did so, and off they went. The animals kept singing, "Up the ladder, down the ladder, there's a chest that's full of adders." When they arrived, her mother was waiting for her near the house. She was glad to see her daughter bring such a nice chest full of treasures. She rushed to the chest and opened it but saw nothing but adders, lizards, and water snakes. She wanted to run away, but the adders attacked her and ate her.

She wanted to run away but could not escape the adders.

THE GIRL AND THE PRINCE IN THE COW'S SKIN

Once upon a time, there was a father who had three daughters. He fell ill, and it occurred to him that water from a well outside of the village could heal him. So he told his daughters, "If I could drink some water from the well, I would feel better at once." His eldest daughter replied, "I will bring you some, Father."

She went out of the village to the well; but as soon as she bent down to draw some water, something shouted out of the deep water, "I will not give you any water until you promise to be mine and stay with me!"

The girl was scared, "What is it? I cannot see a thing, and I do not know who you are. Tell me! Who are you?"

Having come home, she said, "I can't get water from the well, Father." The second daughter replied, "If you can't, I'll go and bring some!"

Yet, the same happened to her, and she did not draw any water either. The third and youngest girl went to the well. When she came to it, something shouted, "If you swear to be mine, you will draw some water, and your father will recover." She replied, "I swear."

The girl drew some water, took it to her father; he recovered at once, and everybody was happy. In the evening, when darkness fell, an ugly creature in a cow's skin came at knocked at their door. The youngest daughter was scared; but what could she do?

She had to open the door. The creature sang a weird song,
Do what you promised
When taking my water;
You are to be mine,
So do let me in!

The girl let him in and gave him something to eat. When everybody went to bed, the ugly creature took off the cow's skin, revealing a young lad who was more handsome than anybody in the world. When midnight came, he put on the cow's skin again, for he had to return to the well. The next evening, he came again. The girl was not afraid anymore and opened the door gladly. He told her that he was a spellbound prince and that she could break the spell if only she did not tell anybody.

The girl could not resist telling everything to her mother. On the third night, her intended one came again. Her mother pretended to have gone to sleep and waited for him to take off the skin. She grabbed it and threw it into the stove. The prince ran about the house, screaming, "How awful! Where is my skin?"

Her mother heard him shouting, came running to them, and confessed to have thrown the skin into the stove. When they took it out, it was too late—the heat had curled it up. The two of them did their best to help the prince get into it; but it was to no avail. It was a very sad goodbye. The prince told the girl that he would have to suffer a punishment; he was to go beyond the red sea; and she could not find him before she had worn out a pair of iron boots, beaten down an iron-sided cane, and cried a pot of tears. The girl ordered a pair of iron boots, an iron-sided cane, and a pot, and began searching for her betrothed one. She would cry day and night, and her tears would fell into the pot. Once, she went deep into the woods and saw a small hut. She knocked at the door.

An old woman came out and asked, "What do you need, girl?" The girl asked the old woman to let her stay overnight. "I cannot let you in for the night, dear, for my husband Moon does not like strangers. Even if I hid you behind the stove, he would find you as soon as he begins to shine," the old woman replied. The girl implored her, and the old woman let her in. Moon came and shouted outright, "Ew, smells of a human soul! Come clean! Who is here?" "I let a girl in for a night. She is wandering about, searching for her beloved one. Have you seen him, a handsome prince?" "No, I have not. She should go to my brother. My brother Sun shines everywhere; but she will have to walk another hundred miles!"

In the morning, Moon took her out of the forest, showed her the way, and gave her a nut, ordering her strictly to hide it well. She walked and cried, and her tears fell into the pot. At last, she came to a large forest and saw a small hut lit up inside. The girl knocked at the door. An old woman came out and asked, "Who is it?" "It is me. I have been walking around in search of my beloved one, but I cannot find him." "No bird comes here; the moon does not shine here; the wind does not blow here. How come you are here?" "I have beaten off my iron-sided cane; I have even worn off my iron boots and cried a potful of tears; but I cannot find my beloved one. Please let me stay overnight."

At night, the old woman's husband Sun came, lit up the space behind the stove, and said, "Ew, smells of a human soul! Come clean! Who is here?" "I let a girl stay overnight. She is wandering about, searching for her beloved one. Have you seen him, a handsome prince?" No, I have not. She should go to my brother. My brother Wind blows all around the world; he might find something out. He lives a hundred miles away from here!" He saw the girl off and gave her a nut.

She walked and cried until she entered another forest and saw a hut lit up inside. The girl knocked at the door, and an old lady came out again, "Who is it? How did you get there? Neither Moon nor Sun shines here; no hare can get here; how come you are here?" "I am searching for my beloved one.

I have seen Moon; I have seen Sun; Sun sent me here to see Wind, for Wind might find my beloved one." She asked her for a bed behind the stove or anywhere at all.

At midnight, Wind came and shouted, "Ew, smells of a human soul! Tell me who is here!" "A girl is staying overnight; she is looking for her beloved one. Have you seen him?" "I have not, but I will send the storm around the world tomorrow; it might see him." They invited the girl to have supper, and they ate chicken. "Collect all the bones and hide them thoroughly; you will need them," Wind said, giving her another nut, and rushed out as an awful storm. Having come back, he said, "Your beloved one is living in a big castle; but there is another woman with him. Go to him, anyway. Maybe you can find him if you overcome all the obstacles."

The girl went to the castle; there was a large dog guarding it. He gave the bones to the dog, and it let her in. She asked for a job, saying she could even graze geese. In the morning, she drove the geese to a meadow and cracked the first nut. There was a most beautiful silver garment in it. The mistress liked it so much that she asked the shepherd girl to sell it. The girl said, "I will give the garment to you if you let me sit near the master for one night." The mistress agreed; but she gave a magic concoction to the master that made him sleep like a log. The girl talked to him, begged, shouted, and cried, "My dear, sunny, do you remember our pulling the cow's skin together? I have worn off a pair of iron boots, beaten off an iron-sided cane, and cried a potful of tears to find you!"

He would not reply and slept soundly. A guardian was keeping ward under the window. Hearing her reproaches, he wondered what it was about.

In the morning, he told everything to his master. The master guessed that it must be the girl who had broken his spell.

In the meanwhile, the shepherd drove the geese to the meadow again in the morning. She cracked another nut.

There was a garment of gold in it. The mistress saw it again, and she liked it greatly, and the second night was just like the first one, and the guardian took his master what he had overheard again.

On the following day, the girl cracked the last nut—the garment in it was made of diamonds. The prince was more careful that time. When his servants brought him the concoction at bedtime, he pretended to drink but did not even touch it. The goose shepherd came to him in the evening, kissed him, and cried, "My dearest one, sunny, my beloved one, the one who was to be husband! Do you remember our pulling the cow's skin? I ordered a pair of iron boots, an iron-sided cane, and an iron pot; I wore off my iron boots; I beat off my iron-sided cane; I cried a potful of tears; but I could not find you! Now that I have found you, you do not say a word."

The master hugged her, kissed her face happily, and said, "You have broken my spell. You are my mistress now. My people will serve you from now on!"

In the morning, the mistress called for her, "Shepherd, get up and go graze the geese!" The master replied, "There is no shepherd here. There is a mistress, and you will graze geese."

They lived happily together until death tore them apart.

GOLDEN FISH

Once upon a time, there was a man. He had been fishing for forty years in a row but had bad luck.

One day, he cast a net and caught nothing but toads. He cast the net for a second time and saw a fish in it—it was small but golden. The Fish begged him to let her go back into the water, "Please release me. I will give you everything you want," she implored. She begged him so wildly that he could not but let her go.

Having returned home, the man told his wife, "You know, I have caught a golden fish today. I let her go because she begged me so desperately. She promised to do whatever I want." His wife said, "What a fool you are. Go ask her to give us a new wash-tub, for the old one is ruined."

The man went to the sea and stood on the shore, took off his hat, and asked the Fish for a wash-tub. The Fish came out of the water and said, "Go home and do not be upset." He came home to see a new wash-tub near the house. The woman was happy. She thought, "So the Fish might give us more." "Go to her and ask for me to become a landowner and to have a new house."

The man came to the shore and took off his hat but dared not speak. The Fish appeared out of a wave and asked, "What do you want?" He told her what his wife wanted, and the Fish told him to go home. The man went home and saw that there was a new house and that his wife had turned into a rich landowner. She was lazing about and shouting at her workers and servants.

She was still not satisfied. Soon, she said to her husband, "Go and tell your Fish to make me a fine lady with an estate of my own and horses, carriages, and servants at my disposal." The man went to the sea and asked the Fish to do so. Having returned home, he saw his wife wearing a most beautiful gown, her servants at nod, doing nothing.

Even that could not satisfy the fisherman's wife. She sent for him, and said, "I do not want to be a fine lady; I want to be a queen. Go to your Fish and tell her I want a royal palace and to be the queen in it." The man went to the sea, and the Fish made that wish come true. Having come home, he saw his wife wearing a crown and surrounded by ladies and gentlemen, servants and armed guardians. The guardians asked him what he wanted. He said he wanted so see his wife, pardon, the Queen. They merely laughed at him; his wife would not give him a glance. She told her people to send him away and even set dogs on him.

For as long as a week, his wife enjoyed herself with kings only. When the week had passed, she sent for her husband, and said, "I have too few servants; go and tell the Fish to be my maid." The man was afraid, but how could he help it? He came to the sea, took his hat off to the Fish, and told her about his wife's fancy.

The Fish did not say a word. She wagged her tail from side to side and disappeared into the waves. The man looked at the waves for a while and finally went home.

What did he find there? The royal palace, the servants, and the ladies and gentlemen were gone; their old hut stood near the forest as it used to do, and his wife was sitting at the threshold, mending a torn fishing net, and crying.

GOLD TROT

Once upon a time, a king went hunting and caught a gold trot. Having come home, he locked her in a special room, and gave the key to his wife, ordering her not to let anybody come to the room. He sent messengers to other kings, inviting them to admire his catch. Somehow he had to leave on business.

The king had an only son. Hardly had his father left the palace when the boy stole the key from his mother's pocket and opened the room where the trot was locked. The animal leaped out and ran to the woods.

The king returned; the guests began coming, too. The king took the key, opened the room, and saw that the trot was not there. The king was outraged. He ordered his wife to get packed, get into a carriage, and go away from the palace, for he thought it was she who had given the key to someone. Hearing it, she fainted.

His son came up to the king and said, "Dear Father, it is no fault of my mother; I did it. I wanted to see the trot and opened the door, and she ran away." His father replied, "Then you will have to suffer the punishment!" The boy begged him, "Father, please do not curse me. Just give me a carriage, a coachman, and a couple of horses. I will go away and never come back." The kings who had come to see the trot admired his request deeply and spoke to the king, "The boy is judging himself fairly. Give him what he asks for and let him go."

A carriage appeared; the boy got into it. The king ordered the coachman to take his son over the hills and far away, forbidding his to come back and bring the boy home. They set off. They went on and on until they reached a place where there was nothing but mountains and valleys, and not a single village nearby. The horses were exhausted with heat and could barely breathe.

The prince and the coachman were awfully thirsty, too, but they could not get a drop of water. At last, they found a well with a bucket near it. There was no sweep, though. They used the reins to tie the bucket and put it down into the well. But the reins were too short to draw water. They took off their belts and tied them together with the reins to make them longer. They were still too short. They discussed which of them should go down into the well. The coachman said, "You should go!" "If I do, you will not be able to pull me out," the prince said. "I will; please go." The prince went down with the help of a rope, filled the bucket, then drew another, and more…

The horses were thirsty enough to drink six buckets each; the coachman nearly drank a whole bucket. Having had enough, he said, "You sit in there; I am leaving!" The boy burst into tears and begged him, "Pull me out! Go alone if you want, just pull me out!" The coachman replied, "If you swear to give me your clothes and take mine and be my coachman, I will pull you out. Also promise not to tell anybody." "Alright, but you shall be the prince until I arise from the dead and become a living being." The coachman pulled him out, put on the princely clothes, and got into the carriage; the prince took the coachman's rugs, sat on the limber, took the reins, and geed up the horses.

Off they went. They traveled long until they found themselves facing a king's palace. The coachman got out of the carriage and went to see the king, while the prince drove the horses to the sheds, unharnessed them, and gave them something to eat.

The king had a beautiful daughter. Seeing the prince dressed up as a coach, she liked him more than his master. The former coachman liked the princess enough to become eager to marry her. He had been staying at the palace for a long time; he was only afraid lest the prince should reveal his secret. He wanted to get rid of the boy.

The princess was always around the sheds, for she wanted to talk to the boy, even though he had said himself to be a peasant son. Having found it out, the coachman told the king, "Most Illustrious Lord, my coachman can make horses grow manes, tails, and hooves of gold. The king was glad to know it, "Oh, how wonderful!" He sent for the prince and brought twelve horses that had never run freely. The king said in a fierce voice, "Get a whip and take the stallions! Make sure they have tails, manes, and hooves of gold when you drive them back in the evening." The prince begged in a tearful voice, "How can I do it?" "You had better do what I tell you to, for if you do not, you shall die."

The prince took the stallions along and walked away, weeping hard. The horses vanished before he knew. The prince came to the forest and found no hoof prints. He sat down under a bush and grieved.

All of a sudden, he saw the trot he had let out. She said, "Hello, my Prince!" "Hello, Golden Trot! I am in trouble because of you—I am to drive twelve stallions with tails, manes, and hooves of gold to the palace tonight. I do not know what to do." "Well, you need not grieve! Sit here and wait for me. I will come to you tonight. Evening came, and he saw the Gold Trot running his way. "Good evening, Prince!" "Good evening, Gold Trot!" The trot made a powerful whistle, and the stallions gathered around them. She blew at each, and their manes, tails, and hooved turned gold. She spoke to the prince, "Ride one of them; the rest will come along."

The prince mounted one of the horses and rode. The palace was far away when the king saw him; he rushed out to see if the horses really had manes, tails, and hooves of gold. He saw that everything was radiant with genuine gold. Looking at them out of the palace window, the coachman was very anxious to see the horses.

In the morning, he came to see the king again and said, "Most Illustrious Master, you have three oxen that have never been in the open. My coachman tells he can make them turn gold." The king ordered his people to set the oxen free; they rushed to the woods, roaring wildly. He sent for the boy again, "Get a whip and go after the oxen! If you fail to bring them tonight, turned to gold, you shall die!" Willy-nilly, the prince went where he was told to go. He entered the woods and could not trace the oxen. He sat under the bush and cried. Finally, he fell asleep with grief.

All of a sudden, the Gold Trot appeared again and shouted to the boy, "Hello, Prince!" "Hello, Gold Trot! You see, I am in trouble again because of you." "I know it well; you need not be upset! Sit here and wait for me; I will come tonight." The prince sat there waiting for her. When evening came, he saw the Gold Trot running his way. "Good evening, Prince!" "Good evening, Gold Trot!" The trot whistled, and the oxen gathered around them. She blew at them, and the oxen turned to pure gold. She spoke to the boy, "Take one by the rope; the rest will follow you. Something makes me think it is not yet the end of your misfortune. But you have saved me from death; so I am going to help you, too. Keep the ring—whenever you rub it against your clothes, you will have whatever you like. Hide it thoroughly lest you should lose it or have it stolen."

The prince thanked the Trot, said goodbye to her, and drove the oxen to the cowshed. The shed was lit up at once as if a fire had started.

The palace people came running to admire it; only the coachman was biting his fists with anger and fear. Therefore, it occurred to him, "I have to drive the prince to his grave, or else I will get into trouble." In the morning, he came to the king again and said, "They say there is a jail where adders eat every prisoner. My coachman boasted his not being afraid of it. How can we see if it is true?"

The king followed the coachman's advice and ordered his people to put the prince to that prison. The prince wrang his arms with fear, but, fortunately, he thought of the ring the Trot had given him, so he entered the cellar bravely.

The princess was very reluctant to marry the coachman pretending to be a prince. She wanted to marry the one in prison, for she loved him and pitied him, and longed for him badly.

Once, she came to the king and said, "Father, let us go to the prison and see if the coachman is still alive." "How foolish you are," the king replied, "there is nothing but bones left of him."

The princess did not believe him and went to the prison by herself. She stood at the door and suddenly heard some music. She pushed aside the stone at the door and saw the prince sitting at the table with no trace of adders around; servants were fussing around him, bringing him fine dishes and drinks. The princess opened the door, entered the cellar, and spent several days in it before returning home. She went to see the king straightaway; he asked her, "Where have you been so long?" "Oh, my aunt came, so I got into her carriage and went to her home. Now that I am back I would like you to do me a favor and take me out for a while."

The king consented, and they went for a walk. His daughter turned to the road that lead to the prison and said in a soft voice, as if she were talking to herself, "The coachman must have got out of lock."

The king wanted to know what had actually happened. He came to the cellar and moved the stone aside. He heard music playing and came in along with his daughter. There was plenty of food and drinks in there; they ate to their heart's content, and then took the prince out and brought him to the palace. The coachman was petrified to see the prince.

The prince came up to him and said, "You were the prince until I rose from the dead. As you can see, I am alive, and this shall be the end to your guile. I will be the prince again!"

He went to the king and told him the story. They sent the coachman away; and the prince married the princess. I drank beer at their wedding. It ran down my mustache but never went in my mouth.

HEALING WATER

A king had three sons. The youngest was said to be a fool; while the eldest and middle ones were thought to be clever.

Once, the king fell ill. The elder sons decided to go and look for healing water that cured all ails and asked their father to let them go. The youngest one wanted to go along, but they would not let him. Yet, he did not ask for permission but took his horse and set off. He entered a forest and stopped at a crossway, not knowing which path to take.

The Wolf emerged out of nowhere and said, "I am going to eat you!" The fool replied, "If you have to eat me, you had better eat my horse." He got off his horse, and the Wolf ate it. He said, "If you do not go now, another wolf, my brother, will come and eat you!" The boy replied, "I will not go on foot. You have eaten my horse. Now you are to carry me!"

He mounted the Wolf, and he brought him across the woods to the Wolf King, who was sitting in the forest by the fire, surrounded by other wolves. The Wolf King asked the boy, "Why did you come to the forest riding a wolf? Where is your horse?" He replied, "The Wolf ate my horse on my way for healing water to cure my ill father." The Wolf King took out a handkerchief embroidered with gold and silver, gave it to the boy, and said, "Mount the wolf that ate your horse again, and let him take you to the Bear King. Hide the handkerchief in a safe place, for you will need it!" The Wolf took him to the Bear King, who was also sitting in the woods by the fire with many bears around him. The Bear King asked the boy, "What do you want in the woods? Bears will eat you here!" "Your Lordship, I am searching for healing water for my sick father!" "Alright, I will help you. Take the ring and put it on your finger to remember about it. I will give you a bear to carry you to the lions. They might tell you something about the healing water. We have no idea where it can be."

The bear brought the boy to the Lion King and asked him, "Do you have healing water?" He replied, "No, there is no healing water here, but we know a thing or two about it. You can find it behind the red sea, where an empty castle stands, in which a princess who has never seen a man lives. There is a cave full of snakes and adders; the water you are looking for runs in the cave." The Lion King gave the boy a gold pin, saying, "Hide it safely, for you will need it," and called the lion who was to take the boy behind the red sea.

The boy mounted the lion and got to the castle in which the princess lived. He spent there several days, waiting. Once, the maid happened to tear the princess's handkerchief while helping her get dressed. She wept and looked for somebody to help her. The fool heard her, went out of the room where he had been hiding, and told her that he was going to help her soon. When the maid came again, the boy gave her the handkerchief the Wolf King had given him and kept the torn one.

After several days, the same maid came to the boy and said her mistress's ring to be broken, asking him to fix it. "Why not?" he replied. The maid gave the ring to the boy; when she came to him again, he gave her the ring the Bear King had given to him and kept the broken one. The princess said she had never seen such a beautiful ring and wanted to know who made it. The maid said, "There is a boy in here who looks for healing water; he made the ring."

When the princess's golden belt pin was broken, she ordered the maid to get it fixed. The boy kept the pin, sending her the one given by the Lion King. The princess asked again, "Who made the beautiful thing?" The maid replied, "The one who is expecting to get healing water." "Even though I must not look at a single man, I would love to see this one, even through three glass doors!"

They sent for the boy, and he stood in front of the door. Seeing him, the princess liked his appearance so much that she ordered her people to open the door and invited the boy to dine with her at once. She was nice to him and gave him a magic potion that made the adders and water snakes in the cave slither away at once. He drew healing water for his father and returned to the princess's castle.

She gave him a magic ointment that could make a dead man come alive again, a finger cut off grow again, and a wound heal. She gave him plenty of money, slaves, and horses. Nothing prevented him from going home now. They set off and traveled until they saw a wayside inn.

His two brothers were there, barehanded, returning to their father with no healing water. They were surprised to see him, "How did our foolish brother get here? So rich! He left home as a poor man but is bringing silver and gold!" He greeted his brothers, ordered the innkeeper to serve food and drinks to them, and his brothers could see that he was living in abundance.

The following day, the three of them set off. The servant noticed the brothers to have devised something mean; so he slowed down to get behind them. He had the magic ointment and money. The prince was carrying the healing water.

As soon as they entered a forest, the elder brothers attacked the younger one, cut off his head, dragged him off his horse, and threw him into the bushes. The boy lay there until his servant arrived. Seeing what had happened, he took out the ointment, applied it to his master's neck, and his head was glued to the body at once.

The two murderers rushed to their father, carrying the healing water that they had stolen from their brother. One of them stretched the water out to his ill brother, while the second one stood behind him at a short distance lest his father should see his cut finger—his brother cut it off back in the forest. All of a sudden, the youngest brother came safe and sound. The elder brothers were afraid but gave no signs of it.

The fool's father told him, "See, they have brought me healing water. What have you got for me?" "Father, it is me who brought the water!" "How come? Where is it?" "My brothers killed me in the woods and took it from me. Can you see the wounds on my neck, Father?" Looking closely, his father understood he was telling the truth. At last, the two brothers admitted everything. When the middle son showed his cut finger, the fool said, "I have an ointment for you. If you apply it to the wound and attach your finger, it will grow alright. No need to call the doctor."

After a short while, the princess sent a servant of hers for the one who had come for healing water. She ordered him to lay half the road with carpets. The eldest brother, who was the most envious and the greediest of them, rushed to the castle and claimed to be the one who had drawn healing water. They let him in. Yet, the princess realized that he was playing a trick on her and said, "It was not you who came here for healing water!" He was drummed out of the castle.

In the meanwhile, the youngest brother set off. He arrived at the castle and showed the princess's handkerchief, pin, and ring to her; she recognized him at once. He brought the princess to his father and married him; and his father gave them his kingdom.

PRINCE AND HIS HELPERS

A king had three sons—two were smart, and one was foolish. In his garden, the king had an apple tree on which gold apples grew, but only as few as three per year—one apple for each son.

Once, the apples began to disappear, and nobody knew where they were. The eldest son was going to watch his apple; he came to the garden and ran around the apple tree the whole evening; but he dropped off to sleep around midnight. When he woke up in the morning, the apple was not there. The following night, the younger son went to the garden, and the same happened to him. On the third day, the youngest son, the one who was thought to be foolish, said, "I am going to watch the apple tree now."

His brothers said, "We could not prevent the theft; you will fail, too. The apple will disappear again." But he put on his coat, went to the garden, lay down under the apple tree, and fell asleep. He woke up about midnight, grasped at the apple, and waited. At midnight, he could hear a noise, as if a gaggle of wild geese was flying.

Looking at the sky, he saw a wonderful boat floating in it. Having reached the apple tree, it stopped. Two men got out of it. They shared a single eye. The first man spoke to the second one, "Give me the eye!" He did. The fool, who was hiding there, stretched out his arm through the branches and took the eye. The second one asked, "Did you take the eye?" The first one replied, "Did you give it to me? Stop kidding me!" The second man insisted, "I did give it to you! There might be someone else here; he must have taken it." The fool spoke, "I got you! I will not give you the eye until you give me all the apples you have stolen." He gave the eye to the first man, forcing the second one to stand near him. The first man got into the boat and took off. After as little as an hour, he brought the apples back. He emptied the bag onto the ground and had to give the boat to the fool as a ransom. The two men had to walk home.

In the morning, the elder brother ran to the garden to see how the youngest one was doing. Having seen him, they rushed to the palace, shouting to the king, "Dad, it is so strange! He is sleeping in some kind of a cradle!" They took their father to the garden and saw the fool sleeping in the boat with the apples scattered around him. He woke up at once and gave the apples to his father, keeping only the one he had been watching on the apple tree.

After a while, he asked his father to let him go over the hills and far away to see what was going on in the world. His father let him go.

The boy got into the boat, gave rudder, took off, and flew high over the woods.

Lowering the boat a little, he saw a man as thick as a barrel lying on the ground and drinking from every puddle. The prince lowered the boat even more and shouted, "What are you doing?" "I am so thirsty that I have to drink from every puddle I find. I have drank three hundred barrels of beer, and I still am thirsty." "Would you mind joining me?" "Why not?" "Get into the boat!" He did, and they floated on until they saw a man lying on the ground and gulping every bone he could find.

They asked him, "What are you doing?" "I have to eat whatever I find, because I am starving. I have eaten three hundred fat oxen, but I am still hungry..." "Would you mind joining us?" "Why not?" "Get into the boat!" He did, and they floated on until they saw a man pressing his ear to the ground. They asked him, "What are you doing?" "Counting the grass that has grown in the day. My master told me to." "Can you hear the grass growing?" "I can, because the grass makes a cracking sound when it grows." "Would you mind joining us?" "Why not?" "Get into the boat!" He did, and they floated on until they saw two men standing.

One was aiming a shot at a hawk—the hawk was soaring high over the woods. He shot the bird dead. The second one ran swiftly and brought the bird in no time. The prince asked them to get into the boat, too. They floated on until they saw a high mountain. Something was roaring and flashing there; a cloud of smoke was hanging over the ground. Looking down, the prince saw two men standing on the mountain and waving their hands. He shouted down to them "What are you doing?" "Mixing the air to make a thunderstorm, for we are tired of fair-weather days." "Would you like joining me?" "Why not?" "Get into the boat!" He took them on board, and they floated on. The storm stilled.

They floated on and on until they saw a big town. They got down onto the ground and called at an inn. The prince left his friends there and went to the tavern. Having come there, he asked the taverner why green garlands could be seen in every window and flags on every roof. The taverner told him, "Our king's daughter will be choosing her groom today. In the afternoon, she will stand at the window. Princes and king's sons who have come from every side will walk by the window, and the one on whom she throws her garland will be her husband." "Can I go and have a look?" "Of course, you can."

The Prince went to the castle, stopped at a distance, and watched. Noblemen came in crowds, got out of their carriages, and walked one by one to the window. As they passed by for the first time, the princess did not throw her garland. They passed by for a second time, but she did not throw it again. Her father came up to her and asked why she was still holding the garland. The princess replied, "Not everybody has walked by! One is standing near the wall."

People ran up to the prince and begged him to walk to the window with the others. He said that he had torn clothes and worn off boots, for he had been traveling for a long time. They insisted, and he had to agree. They walked for a fourth time; he was walking last. As he was passing by the window, the princess threw her garland on him, choosing him to be her husband and the king.

Those who had come to propose envied the prince greatly—how come a total stranger became the king? They told him that he must bring a document from his father stating who he was and where he came from within a day and a night. The prince asked if he could send somebody else. "Yes you can," they said. He turned to the gate and called the one who had brought the dead hawk, "Can you return within a day and a night?" the prince asked him. "Why not?"

He set off at once and was nowhere to be seen within five minutes. Before the prince knew, the runner reached his father's house, got the document, and ran back. It was too early to return; so he lay down under a pear tree and fell asleep. Seeing that there was only a quarter of an hour left, the prince grew anxious.

The one who had been listening to the grass growing lay onto the ground, pressing his ear to it, said, "I can hear him snoring under a pear tree fifteen miles away from here!" The archer said, "I will shoot at his boot button to wake him up." He did. The runner sprang up and, seeing it was late, rushed to the palace so wildly that he was there five minutes before the deadline.

Fine. But the gentlemen said, "One needs a drink after such exercise. If you can drink three hundred barrels of beer, you will be the king." "Can somebody else do it for me?" the prince asked. "Yes." The prince went to his boat, calling the man who had been drinking from puddles, told him the story, and asked, "Can you drink that much?" "Why not?"

They brought three hundred barrels of beer to a large smooth field, told guardians to prevent anybody from helping, and felt the man there for the night. When they came in the morning, the man had drank all the barrels and was finishing the froth in the glasses.

They told the prince, "You win. But you will have to eat three hundred oxen before you can become the king." The prince went to the boat, called the insatiable man, and brought him to the palace.

They brought three hundred oxen to the field and ordered the guardians to watch. When they came on the following day the man was sucking on bones. The gentlemen were outraged; they did not know what to do. So they went home with their troops and waged war on the kingdom. The princess's father got scared; he came to his son-in-law and said, "What can we do, my son? The enemy has surrounded the town, and I have so little troops. What can I do?" "You need not get upset, Father!"

He went to his boat again to call the two men he encountered last and said, "My dear sworn brother, we are in great trouble. The enemy has surrounded the town. Help me! Take the boat, go into the sky and make a huge thunderstorm over the enemy."

The two men got into the boat and took off to the clouds. They waved their hands hard. An awful thunderstorm began; everything roared and flashed; nobody could see a thing. The troops were scared; fear made soldiers' hair stand on end; and they hurried home.

The denied grooms had to leave the prince in peace. The kind helpers he had brought in his boat came to him and said, "You will not need us anymore. We should go." The prince wanted to give them plenty of money for their help, but they would not take any. He thanked them sincerely and said goodbye to them.

He became the king at the edge of the world, where the river had dried, near the marshy stream. I walked there collecting bedtime stories, and I am going to come there again soon. This is the end.

ABOUT THE COCKEREL

A housewife had a cockerel and a hen. Whatever the Cockerel found, he shared with the Hen.

Once, he found a gold wedding ring on the road; the Hen said, "You share everything with me. Why not share the ring?" The Cockerel replied, "I cannot break it into halves; it is too hard." The Hen said, "So let us go to the smith; he can cut it into halves."

A landowner had just brought a horse that needed shoeing when they came. Seeing the Cockerel holding a gold wedding ring in his beak, he called his footman and ordered him, "Go and take the ring from the Cockerel."

The footman did take the ring from the Cockerel. He jumped into the carriage and was about to start. However, the Cockerel sprang on the limber before the coachman lashed the horses, and shouted at the landowner, demanding his ring back.

When the landowner got home, the Cockerel was there. Entering his room, the master saw the Cockerel waiting for him on the table. The Cockerel shrieked, "Give back my ring, Master, give back the gold ring!" The landowner called his footman and commanded, "Grab the foolish Cockerel and throw him into a well to drown."

The footman caught the Cockerel, threw him into the well, and shut the lid close. The following day, the landowner told his footman, "Go and check if the Cockerel is drowned." The footman did so. Having come back, he said the well to have dried. There was not a single drop of water and no cockerel in it. The Cockerel had drank all the water.

He came to the landowner's room again and shrieked, "Give back my ring, Master!" The landowner told his footman, "Take the fool, heat the stove, and throw him in! We are going to have roasted cockerel for lunch."

The footman took the Cockerel, put it into the stove, and shut the stove damper closed. But the Cockerel did not burn, for he poured out the water he had drunk in the well and put out the fire. After a while, the landowner ordered his footman to check if the Cockerel was roasted. Hardly had the footman opened the stove when boiling water burst out into the kitchen and onto the footman, and the Cockerel flew into the room and shrieked, "Give back my ring, master! Give back the gold ring, Master!"

Even though the landowner was gasping with rage, he was scared to see that he could do no harm to the Cockerel and that he had lost his money. He threw the ring to the Cockerel, saying, "Throw the fool out of the door along with the ring!"

The Cockerel grabbed the ring, went to the kitchen, and shouted at the mistress, demanding her to spread a quilt on the floor for him. The mistress said, "No way! I am not going to spread a quilt for you. You have done enough damage!" The master came in, saying, "Do spread the quilt; we will see what comes next."

As soon as the quilt was spread, the Cockerel jumped into its center and poured out all the money, for he had got his ring back. The master and his mistress were so happy to have their money back that they threw a lavish ball to celebrate the occasion. They invited many guests, and the Cockerel dined with them like a human being. At last, he returned to his Hen.

THE FISHERMAN'S SON AND THE WATER MAN'S DAUGHTER

Once upon a time, there was a dog poor fisherman, who had a wife and several children. He went fishing to a lake and sold the fish; but he had to provide as much fish to the lake owner as the latter liked for that.

When the lake owner's family was expecting a visit, they ordered the fisherman to catch plenty of fish. He went to the lake and spent the day setting nets but did not catch a single fish. He could not catch a thing on the following day either.

He went to his master and said that fish would not catch. The landowner was outraged, "I do not care! If you do not bring me fish, I will dismiss you and send you away."

The fisherman went fishing on the following day, too, and nothing was caught. All of a sudden, he was facing a young boy wearing a red shirt. It was the Water Man, who lived on the lake bottom. He spoke to the fisherman, "If you give me your eldest son, you will catch plenty of fish not only today but whenever you like. Only you will have to sign the agreement with blood from your second finger." What could the fisherman do? He agreed.

The Water Man cut his finger, and the fisherman signed the agreement. As soon as he set the net, it was full of fish. Sad, he returned home. His wife asked him, "You have caught so much fish; why are you upset?" He told her that he was to give his eldest son to the Water Man in a week."

A week passed; the fisherman brought his son to the lake, weeping hard. The Water Man surfaced to take the boy under the water. Under the water, there was a glass palace, in which the Water Man lived with his wife, daughter, and servants. They told the boy that they wanted him to play with the Water Man's daughter. If he was nice and polite, he would be allowed to visit his parents.

Janek, which was the boy's name, liked it there, but he grew homesick. Seeing it, the Water Man let him go home for a single day, saying, "Watch out, for if you do not come back, your family will die in water—you, your brother and your mother, and your siblings!" The boy ran home happily, told his family how fine the living was in the Water Man's palace, and came back under the water. He came home every once in a while.

Several years had passed, and the Water Man's daughter had grown up when she told Janek that she would love to live on land, among human beings. When her parents were out, she took the best of the underwater treasures, and the two of them escaped from the water palace. They got on land and ran as swiftly as they could. Looking back, they saw her mother hurrying after them with a most powerful army.

The girl turned herself and Janek into magpies, and they landed onto a tall oak tree. Her mother ordered her warriors, "Shoot the he-magpie, but do not touch the she-magpie!" Yet, they escaped the bullets.

They took off the oak; the girl turned into a hare; and Janek turned into a fox, and started chasing the hare. The girl's mother ran after them, shouting "Shoot the fox, but do not touch the hare!" The shooters missed again. The girl lashed the ground, and a small pond emerged there.

She turned into a she-duck, and he became a he-duck. Her mother shouted, "Shoot the he-duck, but do not touch the she-duck!" Arrows screamed, and the two of them went under the water.

The princess's mother died of sorrow, and the army returned to the underwater palace. Janek and the girl traveled on until they reached the capital. The city was at war, and the king was about to march his troops off.

Janek had to join the royal army, and the girl had to make her living as a servant until the army came back after the war, and Janek returned to her. He was so dexterous at war and became so famous that the king promised to marry his daughter off to him. Janek was very happy and forgot the Water Man's daughter completely.

The king gave a lavish wedding feast. Guests came in crowds; musicians played; Janek sat next to the king and the princess. All of a sudden, a dove and a hawk flew into an open window. They flew around the hall and landed onto a cupboard.

The dove said, "Do you remember my leaving my father's house to take you out of the water, Janek?" "I do!" Janek replied. "Do you remember my mother running after us and my turning you and me into magpies?" "I do!" The guests were puzzled, but the dove went on, "Do you remember our being a couple of ducks on a pond and my mother's dying of sorrow?" "I do!" "Do you remember promising me to love me forever?" "I do!" The groom was very pale, and something strange was happening to him.

The king and his guests sprang up to save him, asking what was wrong. Janek replied that the dove was telling the truth. The feast was ruined.

The dove flew away, and Janek rushed after her and apologized. She turned into a girl, and soon guests came to celebrate the wedding of the Water Man's daughter.

BOY AND HIS DOG AND CAT, AND THE LION CUB

Once upon a time, there was a widow who had a son. She lived in poverty and starved all the time; she wore rags. When she had to go to the field and work from dawn to dusk, she had nothing to lunch on.

One day, the widow told the field supervisor, "I will not go to the field again, for I have nothing to eat, and I cannot work when I am hungry." The supervisor took out his purse and gave her one and a half gold piece so that her son could go to town and buy some bread.

The lad took the money and headed for the town. On his way, he encountered a man carrying a small dog. The lad asked him, "Where are you taking your dog?" "I am going to drown it," the man replied. The lad said, "Please do not drown it. Sell it to me!" "Well, buy it," the man replied. The lad gave him one and a half gold piece, took the dog, and brought it home.

While his starved mother was working in the field, he was playing with the dog. Having returned home, his mother saw that there was no bread. She asked her son, "What did you spend the money on?" "Oh, Mom, I bought myself a dog.". The mother grabbed a whip and gave her son a beating.

On the following day, the same thing happened. The supervisor gave the lad one and a half gold piece, ordering him to buy nothing else and to fetch some bread. On his way to town, the lad saw a man carrying a cat. The lad asked him, "Where are you taking your cat?" "I am going to drown it." "You had better sell it to me!" "So buy it!" The lad gave him one and a half gold piece and went home to play with the dog and the cat.

Returning from the field, his mother had nothing to eat again. She questioned her son what had happened to the money and gave him a beating. She was still hungry.

On the third day, as the supervisor ordered women to work, she told him that her son had not bought anything to eat. The supervisor told him off and asked, "Why did you not buy anything?" "I pitied the cat and did not want the man to drown it." The supervisor gave him one and a half gold piece for a third time and ordered him not to buy a thing but bread for his mother. On his way to town, the lad encountered a man carrying a little lion to drown it. The same happened again. The boy gave the money for the lion. Now he had a cat, a dog, and a lion.

Having come home, his mother gave him a hard beating and sent him away, telling him to take his animals along. The lad walked and walked until he came to a forest.

All of a sudden, he saw an old lion, who was going to take the lion cub from him. The boy wept even more bitterly than he did when his mother was beating him. The old lion said, "Give me the cub, and I will give you a ring that will make all of your wishes come true." The boy agreed, took the ring, gave the cub to the old lion, and walked on.

He walked and walked until he felt hungry. He looked at the ring, saying, "I want to have potatoes and cabbage right here right now!" At that very moment, potatoes and cabbage emerged in front of him. Having eaten his full, the lad along with the dog and the cat walked on along.

Having crossed the forests, he found himself in the fields. Looking around, he saw a splendid palace at a distance. He looked at the ring and said, "I want a better one!" A palace sprang up at once.

The following morning, people were astonished to see a most splendid palace where a smooth field used to lie at the fringe of the forest. They informed the landowner, who lived in the near village. The landowner could not believe it; so he sent his footman to have a look. Returning to his master, the footman said, "Indeed, Master, there is a palace, which is even better than yours!"

The landowner traveled to see the palace himself and realized that it was the truth. He along with his household master and more people went to the palace. They came in. The interior was most beautiful and elegant.

They entered the hall and found nobody but the lad, who was sleeping, and his dog and cat. He woke up, rose from the sofa, and greeted the landowner and his people. The landowner asked him, "Who are you?" "I am a poor orphan and have nobody." "Who built the palace then?" "I did," the lad replied.

The landowner ordered his people to send him away. They grabbed the boy, kicked him out of the palace, and took to the village. Having collected himself a little bit, the boy looked at the ring and said, "I want the palace to disappear without a trace."

Before the landowner knew it, there was nothing but the empty smooth field at the place. The landowner grew angry and took the ring from the lad. He ordered his people to dig a fifteen meter well, stone its walls, and put the boy inside. They built a high wall around the well and battened it tightly. The lad was immured in the well.

The dog and the cat sat down near it and discussed how they could help their owner. The cat said, "We have to give him something to eat; or else he will die of starvation." The dog replied, "Where do we get food and how do we put it there?" The cat said, "Run to a butcher's in town, get a piece of sausage or other meat, not raw—humans do not eat raw meat."

The dog ran to town and brought some food. In the meanwhile, the cat found a rope. They tied the food to the rope; the cat climbed the wall and drew the food up, found a hole in the well, and gradually slipped the package into the well.

The cat spoke to the dog again, "We have to rescue our boy. I will go to the palace, steal the ring from the landowner, and bring it here. We will slip it into the well, and the boy will be able to get out. He cannot escape without the ring."

Early in the morning, the cat went to the palace. The landowner had just got up and was beginning to take a bath. He had taken off the ring and put it onto the table. The cat sneaked up to it, snatched the ring, and took to his heels. The dog was anxious to know if the cat had had good luck; so he ran his way. He had to swim across a small river. Swimming with the ring in his teeth, the cat saw the dog.

The dog called for him, "Have you got it?" The cat replied, "I have!" He dropped the ring, and it went splash into the water. They were greatly upset.

The dog said, "You have done your job; it is my turn." He dove and searched the bottom for the ring, and found it. He surfaced and gave the ring to the cat. The latter tied it to the rope, climbed the well, and called to the boy, "Get the ring!"

The boy was very happy; he grasped the ring, tied it off, and put it on. The cat and the dog stepped far back and watched. The boy in the well just said, "I want the wall to disappear!"

The wall was scattered to dust. The boy got out of the well and returned to his mother along with the cat and the dog.

They lived happily ever after.

THE MAN WHO WENT TO ASK THE SUN

Once upon a time, there were husband and wife, both old and very poor. They had nothing but a hut, a tiny cowshed, and a hen on a roost. They did not even know where her laying place was. They looked everywhere for eggs. At last, the husband made up his mind to ask the Sun. He thought, "The Sun shines everywhere and knows everything; he might tell us where our hen lays her eggs."

The man got packed and set off. On his way, he saw the wild Pear Tree that asked him, "Where are you going?" The man replied, "I have a hen, and I do not know where she lays her eggs. So I am going to ask the Sun." The Pear Tree begged, "Oh kind man, please ask something for me. I blossom every year but never produce pears." The man promised to ask the Sun and walked on.

After a while, he saw a hut in the woods. He came in for the night. The mistress asked him, "Where are you going?" The man replied, "I have a hen, and I do not know where she lays her eggs. So I am going to ask the Sun." The woman begged, "Oh kind man, please ask something for me. I have two daughters; both are hard-working and pretty; but nobody is willing to marry them." On the following day, the man set off.

He walked on and on until he saw a large river. He stopped to think of a way to cross it. All of a sudden, the Fish surfaced and asked him, "Where are you going, man?"

The man replied, "I have a hen, and I do not know where she lays her eggs. So I am going to ask the Sun." The Fish begged, "Oh kind man, please ask something for me. Every fish can swim and go to the very bottom of the river; but I can merely float and cannot go down." The man said, "Take me across the river before I do it for you." The Fish carried him across the river; he thanked her, and traveled on.

As he walked on, the sun began to shine brighter and warmer until it even called out to him, "Do not come closer, for it is so hot here that you will burn! I know what you want of me. Listen, your hen lays her eggs on top of the roof, on the very crest of it; it has already laid two dozens of eggs there. Go home and take them. There is money buried under the Pear Tree, who asked you to find out why she produces no fruit—ten carts of money. As soon as somebody digs the money out, the Pear Tree will start producing pears. The reason why nobody wants to marry the girls is that they throw out their garbage facing the Sun, which the Sun cannot stand! As soon as they stop doing it, men will begin proposing to them. The Fish, who wanted to know why she cannot go down to the bottom of the river, will be able to do so as soon as she eats a human being. Only do not tell it to her straightaway; wait until she has carried you across the river and you have walked away a little, for she might eat you. Now you know everything."

The man thanked the Sun sincerely, made a low bow to him, and walked back. When he reached the river, the Fish was waiting for him. The man told her, "Carry me to the opposite bank before I can tell you what I have found out." The Fish carried the man across the river; he stepped away from the water, and shouted, "You have to eat a human being to be able to go to the river bottom!" The Fish darted to catch him, but the man was too far away. She thrashed in the water with rage.

The man reached the hut in the woods and told the mistress what her daughters had to do to get married. The woman was so happy that she wanted to give him a wonderful treat and a present, but the man thanked her and traveled on, for he could not wait to come home.

He walked on and on until he found the Pear Tree. He told her what the trouble was, and she asked the man to dig out the money. He took a horse and a wagon, removed the money, and went home. He and his wife became rich.

Of course, the man managed to find the hen's eggs on the roof.

THE MAGIC GUN, THE FIDDLE, AND THE BOOTS

Once upon a time, there was a wife who had an only son, whom she loved dearly. She wanted her son to be wealthy, but she was very poor and failed to get rich. Whatever she managed to save up she had to spend, so the most she ever had was three groszes. Her son was about to turn thirteen; the widow had nothing but the three groszes for him.

One day, she told her son, "I think I cannot save up any more for you. Take the three groszes and go make your way in life. Maybe you can make yourself a better living." The boy took the money and left.

Passing a town, he felt like buying something. But what can one buy for three groszes? He bought a candle and walked on until he saw a wayside inn. The boy entered the inn and saw nobody but two portrays on the wall. It was getting late; so the boy decided to sleep in the inn.

He broke the candle he had bought into halves, put one half under one of the portrays and the other under the second one, lay down, and fell asleep. Everything was silent; nobody made a sound.

All of a sudden, there was a terrible noise at about midnight. The boy woke up to see three men, handsome and well-dressed, searching the inn for something. Seeing the boy, they shouted, "Come here, boy!" The boy got off the stove and came up to them. The men asked him, "Which portray do you like better?" This or that?" He replied, "I like both alright." They insisted, "Just tell which is better." The boy replied the same, "I find both pretty." They were happy to hear it and said, "If so, you are a smart boy, and we are going to give you something for it."

One of the men gave him a golden gun; another gave him a fiddle that could make everybody dance; and the third one gave him a pair of boots to step a kilometer and jump seven at once. Having taken the presents, the boy thanked them, and left.

He walked on and on until he encountered a landowner in a carriage. The landowner noticed the boy and called out to him, "Come here, boy!" The boy did. "Where did you get the gun?" the landowner asked, for he liked it greatly. The boy replied, "A man gave it to me." "Would you mind selling it to me? I would pay you well." "No way I can sell it" the boy answered." "Does it shoot well?" the landowner asked. "Of course it does. It shoots the aim at any distance. Can you see the eagle soaring so high that I can hardly see it, master?" "Shoot it; let us see if you can kill it." The boy aimed a shot, and shot the eagle dead. The eagle fell down into the thickest reeds at once.

The landowner wanted to take the eagle; but he could not send his coachman there, for he had skittish horses which he could not cope with on his own. Reluctantly, he got out of the carriage and went to get the eagle. In the meanwhile, the boy took out the fiddle, adjusted it, and began to play. Hearing the music, the coachman began to jump on the limber; the horses danced fancily. The coachman felt uncomfortable jumping on the limber, and the dancing horses irritated him; so he jumped off the limber and danced wildly facing the horses and holding their bridles. The boy kept playing, and everything reverberated. The landowner jumped in the reeds, having forgotten the eagle completely.

At last, the musician grew tired and stopped playing. He made a step in his boots and covered a kilometer at once; he made another step, and he was two kilometers away. He jumped, leaving seven kilometers behind him. He walked on unhurriedly.

The landowner could not find the eagle; his clothes were torn, his face scratched, and he was too tired of dancing to walk to the carriage on his own. The coachman pulled him out of the bushes and dragged him to the carriage.

On his way home, the landowner fell awfully ill.

The boy wandered around the world and happened to come to the landowner's estate. He asked a servant to find out if they needed a musician, pretending to be a traveling one. "Alright," the servant said. "I will go and ask; wait here. Our master is ill, but he might want to listen to you playing not to be too bored." The servant came to the landowner's room and asked him, "Illustrious Master, a traveling musician has come and asks if you want him to play the fiddle to you." "Where is he? Call him in!" When the boy entered the room, the landowner was in his bed. Seeing the boy, he recognized him at once and shrieked, "Aha, it is you! I will teach you a lesson!" He called his servants at once, and ordered them to tie the boy up and sent him to jail.

The servants could not help it. They caught the boy, tied him up, and took his gun, leaving him nothing but the fiddle and the boots. The boy sat in the jail, waiting for the trial.

In the meanwhile, the landowner was giving a feast. Crowds of guests came. The landowner told them about his adventure and said that he had the boy in jail—he wanted to take him to court for his mockery. Hearing it, the guests asked the landowner to show the boy to them. His servants went to the jail and brought the boy to the guests. "Here is the wretch that made me cripple myself in the bushes by playing the fiddle."

The guests said, "Alright, you can take him to court, but let him play to us first!" The landowner begged, "I will never let him play! I am too weak; I am bound to depart if I have to dance!" But the guests were in a good mood; they laughed at the landowner and asked him to let the boy play. The landowner would not agree, "He shall not play!"

Yet, seeing that he could not talk his guests out of it, he conceded, "Alright, let him play. Just tie me to my bed to keep me from moving." Servants brought a rope and tied up the landowner as he had ordered." "Let him play," the landowner ordered. He did not have to ask the boy twice.

He hurried to put on his boots, take his fiddle, and begin to play. Ladies and gentlemen nearly danced the room to pieces. They ruined and broke whatever happened to stand in their way, tables and chairs, and kept dancing like mad.

The boy kept playing. The landowner tossed so hard in his bed that it nearly cracked. He somehow managed to free one of his feet, put it onto the floor, and went stamp-stamp-stamp, saying repeatedly, "I told you not to ask him to play! I told you!"

At last, the boy grew sick of playing. He saw that the noblemen could hardly breathe. He grasped the gun, made a one kilometer's step, then a seven kilometers' jump, and escaped.

THE GLASS HILL

Once upon a time, there was a woman who had a household and three sons. Two were smart, and the third one, Bartko, was stupid. She also had three meadows, where thick grass grew, which made perfect hay when dried.

One day, she told her children, "Dear sons, please go to the meadow and scythe the grass. We have to make hay while the sun shines." Her sons went to the meadows.

Having scythed a meadow and a second one, they said, "Let us scythe the third one now." Having come to the third meadow, they saw no glass at all, as if animals had been grazing there.

When the boys came home, their mother asked them if they had scythed the three meadows. "We have scythed two," her sons replied. "Why not three?" their mother demanded. "Somebody has grazed cattle on it." "If so, you will have to guard the meadow so that nobody can pasture cattle on it." "Why not," her sons replied.

After a while, the eldest son went to guard the meadow. The grass was thick and tall; he hid in the shrubs and waited. He lay there until midnight, then fell asleep and slept until 1 a.m. He woke up to see the grass trampled down. He could not but go home.

His mother asked, "How was it? Is the grass there?" "Huh, somebody trampled it down at night again." The grass grew again, and the second son came to guard it during the night.

He fell asleep in the shrubs at about midnight and woke up to see the grass gone.

The foolish Bartko had to guard the meadow on the third night. He took a loaf, a potful of butter, and three pieces of cheese—enough to last him for a week. Evening fell and dusk came; the boy stayed awake watching the meadow. At midnight, three horses appeared out of the old thick oak tree that grew on the meadow and began to graze on the grass. Bartko leaped out of his hide and tried to catch them.

All of a sudden, the horses turned into pretty girls, and spoke to him, "Do not send us away; we are spellbound princesses. If you set us free, you will be the king." The boy brought the food he had taken from home, and gave it to the girls. He would bring them food to the oak tree every night. Once as he brought them bread and cheese, the girls told him, "The king, our father, is going to send letters around the country, declaring that the one who climbs the glass hill will marry the youngest of us, who lives on the glass hill. Come here; we will give you kingly clothes and a horse; you shall get dressed and climb the hill which nobody else can climb. Make sure you do not tell anybody, even your own mother."

Everything was as they told him. The king sent around letters inviting all kings, princes, and noblemen to his palace. The one who climbed the glass hill was to marry the king's daughter. The two smart brothers decided to participate.

They took their best horses and some money, and set off; the foolish one asked his mother to let him go along. "You stupid thing, what are you going to do here? If you go, you will end up in jail!" his mother said. But he begged her wildly, saying that he needed no money but only a small loaf of bread, a little cheese, and some butter.

His mother gave him the food; he took it and went to the oak tree on the meadow, to the girls. One of them turned into a horse, and the other two helped him put on kingly clothes, and the boy looked so handsome that no king or prince could be equal to him. The girls said, "When you have reached the hill top, do not let the servant take the horse; only ask him for a glass of water and a hunk of bread to be polite. Make sure you do not stay longer than an hour! Remember that you need to mount the horse and return to us as soon as an hour passes. Our youngest sister will try to prevent you from doing so; tell her you have to check the horse."

Many people came to the hill and watched Bartko reach the hill top quickly. They wondered who the handsome prince could be. He looked at his watch and went to the palace. The princess was glad to see him and talked to him sweetly, though she had not said a word before. The prince ordered a servant to give the horse a hunk of bread and a glass of water. An hour passed before he knew it. Bartko said he had to check the horse. He came out, mounted the horse, and rode down the hill slope, for it was high time he did so. In the meanwhile, the king ordered his people to lock the gate and catch him to find out who he was. The horse jumped over the gate and across the water, and galloped to the meadow, to the oak tree. It turned back into a girl. Bartko gave back the costly clothes and returned home to his mother.

His brothers returned home and told his mother what it had been like and what they had seen. The foolish brother replied, "Seems like you did not see much!" The prince turned his back on them, looking just the way he did when riding the horse. They wanted to beat him, but his mother said, "Leave him alone, why beat a fool?"

Little time had passed when the king sent letters around for a second time, and guests came from around the world again. The two brothers were going to participate again, and Bartko asked his mother to let him go along. "Why would you go there? Stay at home and do the housework; do not waste the day!" his mother said. Bartko insisted, and she allowed him to go.

Bartko took the same things as he had taken before and went to the oak. Another girl turned into a horse, and the others dressed him even better than the previous time. They told him, "You must not stay longer than two hours this time. Order the servant to give two hunks of bread and two glasses of water to the horse. When two hours have passed, go back. If the princess tries to keep you there, tell her you have to check the horse." He mounted the horse and reached the hill top. The princess greeted him sweetly again. After two hours, he told her that he had to see his horse again and left. In the meanwhile, the king ordered his troops to surround the hill and lock the gate. It was to no avail—the horse jumped over the sentry and the gate, and galloped to the oak tree. Having arrived, it turned back into a girl. The fool gave back the splendid clothes and went home.

His brothers returned home and told his mother what it had been like and what they had seen. The foolish brother could not resist saying, "Seems like you did not see much! Are you trying to say I was riding with my feet up and my head down?!" They wanted to beat him, but his mother said, "Leave him alone, why argue with a fool?"

The king sent letters around for a third—and last—time. Guests began to come again. The two brothers got packed.

The fool persuaded his mother to let him go along and went to the meadow, to the oak tree. The third girl turned into a horse, and the others dressed him finely and gave him advice, "When you are on the hill top, tell the servant to bring three hunks of bread and three glasses of water to the horse. This time you should stay with our sister for three hours before you return to us. If you do so, you will break our spell." Bartko mounted the horse and rode onto the glass hill top. He stayed with the princess for three hours before he said, "I have to check my horse." She would not let him go; she begged him to stay; but he would not listen. He left, mounted the horse, and galloped to the meadow.

In the meanwhile, the king ordered a powerful army to surround the hill, and his warriors caught Bartko.

The lad admitted his being the one who was to break the spell on the king's daughters. He said he had to go to the oak tree, and asked the guests to wait for him. The king consented.

When Bartko reached the meadow, he saw two girls waiting for him, wearing beautiful dresses; and the third one, who had turned into a horse for him, shook off the skin and turned into a pretty girl, too. A carriage appeared out of nowhere, and they got into it.

The girls gave Bartko as many as five carts of treasures. As they were approaching the castle, Bartko lifted a beautiful shiny red flag, and waved it merrily.

Having reached the castle, he came to the king and said, "Here they are, King. I have broken the spell on your daughters." "Fine," the king replied, "you can marry one."

The girls said that he was to marry the youngest sister, the one living on the glass hill.

Bartko married the princess, and nobody called him a fool after that. He lived happily ever after, helping his mother and brothers.

FEAR

Once upon a time, a man had two sons.

Their names were Walek and Wojtek. Walek was just like others—he understood what others understood and did not pretend to be very wise; but everyone called him the smart brother because his brother was a fool. The stupid Wojtek could not understand what fear was. Whenever the elder brother said he had fear, Wojtek would ask him a thousand questions, but he still could not understand a thing. Finally, his brother grew angry and decided to show Wojtek what fear was like.

One autumn day, at dusk, the foolish Wojtek's brother sent him to the tavern for brandy. Walek knew that his brother would be passing a cemetery, which was the shortest way. He sneaked out of the house, sooted his face, wrapped his mother's black skirt around his head, and stood on a path in the very center of the cemetery with a glowing ember in his mouth.

After a short while, Wojtek appeared. Seeing the horrible figure, he shouted, "Hey you! Step off the path! I do not want to walk in the mud..." Walek made the most terrible moan he could. "You dumb?" the fool yelled, coming closer. "Off my way, or else I will tan your hide!" The smart brother thought, "I will make you run away!" Moaning in an even scarier way, he spread his arms open and began approaching Wojtek as if to catch him. He was not even close! Instead of running away, Wojtek lifted his oak stick, jumped at Walek, and started beating him hard. The ember fell into Walek's throat, burning him painfully. The poor thing moaned and moaned, unable to utter a word. He wanted to take off his mother's skirt but got caught in it and fell down into the mud. Wojtek did not recognize him before he had given him about a hundred sticks. As soon as he knew it was his brother, Wojtek apologized, though he was very surprised to see him playing such stupid tricks.

Grinding his teeth with rage and pain, Walek dragged home. Seeing what had happened to his smart son, his father grasped a lash and might have given the foolish Wojtek a hard beating if he had not hidden in the attic and pulled up the ladder. The following morning, poor Walek was very ill. They had to let his blood and cup his back and sides.

Wojtek's father was so mad at him that he would not even ruin his lash; he just sent him away. "Let trouble tell you to be smarter, you fool!" he said. His mother cried, begging her husband to let Wojtek stay, but it was to no avail—the brothers' father would not listen to her.

The fool had to get packed and wander off. His mother gave him a good bag of money, though. "My oh my!" the fool thought on his way, "my father sent me away as if I was a dog! For what? For not knowing what fear is like! If only I could encounter fear just once!"

Having wandered for about a week, the stupid Wojtek called at an inn. When people asked him who he was and where he was going, Wojtek replied sincerely that he did not know where he was going and wanted to know what fear was like. Everyone in the ill roared with laughter. The innkeeper patted Wojtek on the shoulder and said, "If you really need it, it is as easy as that. We can show you what fear is like. Can you see the tall palace on the mountain top over there? It has been empty for ages, for people are afraid to live in it. If you want to feel fear so badly, go and sleep in the palace. You will see what happens." "Of course I will go," Wojtek replied. "If I really encounter fear, I will pay you well for your advice. Just bring some food and drinks there for me. How can I spend the whole night there without eating?"

Seeing that Wojtek was really going to sleep in the palace, the guests and the innkeeper gave up jokes and tried to talk Wojtek out of it, saying that a brave man like he had gone there and never come back. Wojtek would not listen to them; the harder they tried to scare him, the more eager he was to encounter the fear.

At last, everybody gave up trying to persuade him. In the evening, they brought enough firewood to last through the night, several sausages, and a large bowl of bacon and potatoes to the castle. Wojtek said goodbye to everybody in the inn and went to the palace merrily.

In a spacious room with a stove in it, he made a fire, moved and armchair up to it, and put his victuals onto the table. He lit his pipe, made himself snug in the armchair, and listened to the wind roaring in the stove. The roaring was mournful and loud enough to make one's hair stand on end. Wojtek sat there for a while and grew hungry. He played the master. He put the potatoes over the flame, tied the sausages to a wooden stick, and began to roast them. When the potatoes started to simmer and the sausages were shedding fat, something in the stove shouted in a terrible voice, "Flying!" "Damn you! Wait a second; I have to take my supper out," Wojtek replied loudly, putting the bowl under the table and placing the stick with sausages on it over it. "You can fly if you like." Something roared in the chimney and fell right into the flame. Waiting for somebody else to roar in the stove, Wojtek continued to roast the sausage and potatoes. Finally, he put everything onto a plate and placed it onto the table.

Glancing back, he saw a scary-looking bearded man standing behind him silently.

"Hey, friend! Why are you standing silently?" the fool called out. "Get an armchair and sup with me." The scary-looking man took an armchair silently and sat at the table but would not eat. Wojtek invited him several times, but, seeing that he was not listening, took to his supper alone.

When he was finishing the last piece of sausage, the scary-looking guest said in a dull voice, "You have had enough; give me some." "You would not it have when I invited you. I am not going to give you anything now," Wojtek replied, gulping the last piece.

"If so, I will roast you!" the ugly creature roared. "Hold on, brother! You must be Fear. Are you? So why are you foolish enough not to eat when I offer you food? I have been wandering for about a fortnight to meet you. Now that I see how stupid you are I know it was not worth the time!" "I will show you how stupid I am!" Fear yelled, clasping his hands on Wojtek's throat.

Wojtek held his own. He gave the ugly man a couple of fists on the head, knocking him senseless. The man collapsed onto the floor. The fool sat down on his chest, pinning him down to the floor, and said, "Now, brother, which of us is stronger? Your great height did not help you, did it, huh? What will you give me if I let you go?"

"I will give you treasures better than you can dream, not for setting me free, though. I will give them to you for relieving the pain I have been suffering for a hundred years. I have been the master of the castle and to have enormous strength. I have wrestled with many strong men, and I floored them all. They have been torturing me in the castle every night. It was to last until a man defeated me. If you had given me the last piece, I would have taken your strength. Now come with me and take whatever you like."

Wojtek followed the man into a large cellar, which was full of silver, gold, and gemstones. Fear let him take whatever he liked. Wojtek picked only gold and precious stones, though he had never seen any of those. Having taken a heavy load, Wojtek wanted to say thank you to Fear, but the latter was gone.

"Fine! No need to bow!" the fool thought happily and left the palace, bent down under his burden. He hired a cart and went to town. When in town, he bought a lot of beautiful things.

He lived in plenty ever after, and everybody called him smart Walek.

TITELITURY

Once upon a time, there was an ancient castle on top of a high mountain, and a young prince lived in the castle.

The castle was surrounded by thick woods, in which goats, and boars, and shaggy witches lived. The prince enjoyed hunting in the forest more than anything.

One morning, he mounted a horse and rode to the forest. He rode on and on along a forest path. Thrushes were whistling; turtle doves were clanging, and an oriole was chirping on an oak tree.

The path led him through the woods until he reached a glide. Pink, white, and yellow flowers bloomed on the glide, and bees were buzzing over them. Looking around, the prince saw a lake glistening behind the trees; there was a hut on its bank. He saw a green small garden near the hut, rife with sunflowers and red roses. "I wonder who lives in the hut," the prince thought. "I have been in the forest many times, but I have never seen the hut."

He came closer and stopped. The door was open, and he could see a beautiful girl sitting at a spinning wheel in the mud room with a low ceiling, singing silently,

The skylark jumps from stone to stone;
My heart is sick, and oh, I mourn;.
My mother is not here; she died
Leaving behind her orphaned child.
Stepmother got stale bread for me
That I eat sadly in a corner.

Seeing it finished, she says, "Gee! It should last longer!"

Hearing that song, the prince felt sorry for the girl. Suddenly, her stepmother glanced out of the window, saw him, and ran outside. She made a low bow to him and began praising her poor orphan. She praised and praised her, and finally said, "Gracious Master! She can make gold of straw!" "How come?" the prince asked in surprise. "Yes she can! She is a wizard with her fingers! Look, she is spinning gold with this spinning wheel."

The prince took the girl to his house and married her. They lived happily together like a pair of turtledoves.

After a while, the prince came to recall what her stepmother had said about gold. He ordered his people to bring several bundles of straw and call girls from all around the village so that his wife can teach them how to spin.

Hearing it, she burst into tears, hid in a closet and cried in the corner, saying, "Woe is me! Woe is me! Can I spin gold?"

All of a sudden, a disgusting dwarf came out from behind the stove. He came up to her and said, "You need not be upset, Gracious Mistress! I will help you. Take these magic gloves. If you put them on and begin spinning, you will get golden threads. Yet, you are to guess my name. This time tomorrow, I will come and ask you. If you fail to guess, you will have to be my wife."

The pretty girl cried but agreed. The dwarf gave her the magic gloves, which were made of pure gold, turned into a strange-looking bird, and flew out of the open window.

The pretty girl put on the magic gloves, called all the spinners, and sat at her spinning wheel. As soon as she got a handful of straw, golden threads began to appear from under her fingers. "Wow!" a spinner exclaimed in surprise. "Woow!" a second one exclaimed. "Wooow!" the third one exclaimed.

The pretty girl kept spinning the golden thread silently. The prince was hunting in the woods. He had been chasing a deer for a long time and was tired. He jumped off his horse and sat down under an old oak tree. All of a suddenly, a strange bird began to chirp up on the tree,

Sing aloud, my bird sisters; For I am going to have a mistress. A pretty girl sits in a room; Her eyes are bright, her cheeks in bloom. The spinning wheel spins round and round; A golden thread is quickly wound. The beauty is in hell; My name she cannot tell. Titelitury! Titelitury! Prepare your wedding dress; My name you cannot guess. Titelitury! Titelitury!

The prince memorized every word of the song. He cheered up, took his kill, and rode home. His young wife came to meet him halfway. "This is for you, dear!" she said, stretching a ball of golden thread to her husband.

He was very pleased and ordered his people to give the spinners a good treat. At night, he told her wife the song he had heard from the strange bird. She knew at once that it was the dwarf. So that was his name! She memorized it well.

The dwarf came at the time agreed, made a low bow to the pretty girl, and said, "Good day, Gracious Mistress! Remember your yesterday's promise and tell my name." "Your name is Titelitury!" she cried out merrily.

There was a thunderclap. The dwarf flew noisily out through the roof, raising clouds of smoke. The pretty girl span gold ever after, lending her magic gloves to every spinner in the village.

THE TAILOR'S WIFE
AND THE COUNTESS

A long time ago, a tailor named Philipp Waxend lived in a small town. Everybody in the town knew the tailor, because there was a sign over his door, which everybody could see from a distance. There was a huge boot last on it, and it read, "TAILOR PHILIPP WAXEND LIVES AND WORKS HERE."

Tailor Waxend always sat by the window, stabbing leather hard with his awl, sometimes breaking wooden nails he could not insert in warm blood.

The tailor was a hardworking but very quarrelsome man. He also was so greedy that no apprentice could stand him. Not a single day passed without Waxend finding faults with them—one was too cheeky, another did not know how to hold the awl... Nothing could make him pay anybody all he earned. He had to work all alone for weeks and months in a row—his apprentices got sick of him very soon and discouraged others to work with him.

His wife had to work too. The tailor would take it out on her, call her bad names, yell at her, and even punch her. The poor woman was afraid to speak lest they should quarrel again. She did whatever her husband ordered her to do silently. She was a timid kind woman and pitied the poor greatly, perhaps because she had got a raw deal.

A rich nobleman lived in a splendid castle at a lake opposite to the town. Old people said his grandfather to have been a poor fisherman. Once when fishing, he caught treasures in his net. He bought himself the splendid castle and the woods around it along with two lakes.

The young gentleman spent many years abroad and brought a very beautiful wife. As soon as she arrived, she ordered everybody to call her husband "Your Lordship Count," and her "Most Illustrious Countess." Everybody saw how peevish and wicked the Countess was. She beat her maids, punched them, and called them bad names on every pretext. His Lordship Count got a good scolding whenever he said something wrong. Nobody could please the peevish mistress; she did not like anything. People and even the master, her husband, had a horror of her.

One day, a traveler stopped by the castle gate. When the Countess was passing him by in her beautiful carriage, he made a low bow to her and stood in her way. The carriage stopped. The traveler came closer with another bow and asked the Countess to help him find a job. The Countess was struck dumb. She glanced at the traveler silently, then jumped out of the carriage, grabbed the coachman's whip, and began whipping the traveler's bare feet. "How dare you stop my carriage?!" she shrieked, "How dare you speak to me?!" The traveler jumped aside and silently watched the carriage disappear around the corner.

After a while, he went to the town and soon turned into a narrow street leading to the lake. He stopped near a small house, and read the sign on it, "TAILOR PHILIPP WAXEND LIVES AND WORKS HERE."

The traveler rang the bell, entered the workshop quietly, and asked if there was any job for him. However, the tailor was not at home; his wife advised that he ask for a job elsewhere, saying that her husband was very wicked and nobody could stand him, though she pitied the wanderer greatly. "I have nothing but a grosz," she said, "It is all I can give you. The tailor will beat me when he finds out, but I think you need it more than he does. I am not afraid of being beaten, anyway. Take the grosz, and may it bring you good luck."

The wanderer thanked the kind woman, left the workshop, and headed for the lake. He could see the castle on the opposite bank. Looking at it, the wanderer whispered to himself, "I should correct a mistake. May the two women I have met today swap places. May the tailor's wife become the Countess, and the Countess become the tailor's wife." The wanderer was a sorcerer. Hardly had he finished when darkness fell. That night, the Countess found herself in the bed of the tailor's night.

When the tailor's wife fell asleep, she went to the castle. ...After several minutes in a hard bed, the Countess started to toss around. Prickly straw hurt her. The Countess was beginning to simmer with anger. She felt like telling off the servants for making the bed so badly before she even woke up. Her swearing woke Tailor Waxhead, and he sat up listening to his wife. Yet, he could not understand a thing, for the Countess was speaking German. So Waxhead shouted her in the ear, "Hush!.. I will fix you up in no time! Shut your mouth and sleep!" The Countess was scared to death and did not make a sound. What happened? Where is she? It is dark, something is wheezing fiercely like a big bear next to her. The Countess pulled the feather bed over her head, shivering. She fell asleep soon, thinking that she had been dreaming.

In the morning, the tailor found his wife sleeping, all covered with the feather-bed. "Why?! To sleep in broad daylight? Who is to pitch the wax head?" The tailor was outraged. He took a stick, tore off the feather bed, and began to beat the Countess with the stick. The Countess screamed on the top of her lungs, but he kept beating her and calling her names. Finally, he pushed her off the bed. "Go and pitch wax head, now!" Weeping, the scared Countess ran to the door, though she could not quite understand what Waxhead wanted of her.

At that time, the tailor's wife was sleeping soundly. She did not wake up at night—she was warm and comfortable. At last, she opened her eyes and wondered what had happened and where she was. Everything was silent. She could hear something go clip-clop. "Am I dreaming?" the tailor's wife thought. "Am I dead and in Heaven?"

Suddenly, the door opened, and her maid Kasia entered. She stepped silently, wearing nothing but stockings on her feet, fearing lest the Countess should yell at her. She came up to the bed and asked timidly, "Gracious Mistress, which dress shall I prepare for you today?" "Oh! What do I say?" the tailor's wife thought anxiously. Looking at Kasia, she answered in a sweet voice, "Whichever you like, dear." Kasia was surprised to hear her, for the Countess never spoke so nicely to her. She looked at her mistress, and her mouth dropped open. Her mistress's face and hands were smeared with tar.

Kasia backed out of the room and ran to the kitchen, where the slaves were waiting in horror to know in what mood their mistress was that day. "Oh dear! Oh dear!" Kasia whispered, running into the kitchen. "Our Countess must have spent the night in hell. She is all smeared with tar! Something must be wrong, for she is being so very sweet!"

The tailor's wife got up, washed the tar off her hands and face, got dressed, and went for a walk around the castle. In one of the rooms, the master came up to her, greeted her politely, and kissed her hand. He was astonished to see his wife so kind a sweet—she did not shout and swear, she did not stamp her feet. The tailor's wife walked around with him, guessing what might have happened to her.

In the meanwhile, the Countess was sitting in her corner and eyeing the tailor angrily. He was waving a belt over her head and singing a song, "Warm, and safe, and wealthy land — hell is home to noblemen!"

HOW THE SLUG DEFEATED THE FOX

One morning, the Fox got out of his hole and thought, "It is Sunday; I should get something tasty for dinner."

He ran out of the woods to Lake Purda and lay in wait for ducks. There were so many ducks at the lake that seeing them made the Fox's mouth water, and he could not wait for them to come out of the water. He sneaked up to the reeds and hid there.

A flock of ducks approached the reeds to hide in their nests. The Fox leaped into the water and could very well have caught a duck, but it flew up, and the artful Fox went ungifted away. It was that way the whole day. By the time evening fell, the Fox was so sick of the unfortunate hunting that he did not feel like eating duck anymore.

He wandered angrily on a meadow and encountered the Slug. He told the Slug, "Hey little rascal! Where are you going?" "I want to go around the lake until sunset." The Fox burst out laughing and said, "He, he, he! I could run around it, but you?! No way you can cover the way in three days!" The Slug replied, "Willing to compete with me?" "Why not. Only if I cover the way quicker than you do, I will eat you!" The Slug answered calmly, "Agree."

The Fox was glad and eager to start. Yet, the Slug had more to say, "Before we start running, I shall count to three. Stand in advance of me—I can win anyway!" The greedy and proud Fox could not wait and danced on the sand. "Can we go?" "Not yet!" the Slug replied. He glued himself to the Fox's tail and shouted, "One, two, three, off we go!"

The Fox dashed off and ran as swiftly as he could. Having covered half of the distance, he looked back to see no trace of the Slug. The Fox fell down to have a rest and called out, "Where are you, Slug?" "I am here!"

Hearing that, the Fox shoot off and ran at a breakneck pace. The sun had set, and darkness had fallen by the time he reached the place where they had started. He could not see the Slug. He wagged his tail happily.

The Slug came unstuck and shouted, "Have you just arrived? I have been standing here for half an hour waiting for you!" The Fox felt ashamed; he dropped his tail and dragged to his hole, hungry as he was.

CONTENTS

SERMON	5
THREE LAMPS	6
ABOUT A SIMPLE MAN WHO COMFORTED HIS MASTER	11
PEOPLE GETTING RICH	14
DO WIVES LIKE THIS EXIST?	18
THE OWL AND THE HAWK	20
THE REASON WHY THE HARE EATS NO MEAT	21
THE DOG'S WINTER THOUGHTS AND SUMMER THOUGHTS	23
IS THERE JUSTICE IN THIS WORLD?	24
MAZEK'S DEBT	27
VERY WORST PUNISHMENT	30
MARIA: WHAT IS DESTINED TO COME SHALL COME	32
IT DOES NOT STAB, NOR DOES IT SHOOT, YET IT KNOCKS ONE SENSELESS	38
ABOUT A RICH GENTLEMAN	42
HOW A SMITH WORKED HIS WAY TO HEAVEN	44
ABOUT A PRINCE WHO DID NOT WANT TO DIE	46
ANUSZKA THE GOLDEN BRAID	48
A PRESENT FOR THE KINGS' GODSON	51
ABOUT THE KING'S SON	55
HOW A SIMPLE MAN'S SON BECAME THE KING AND MARRIED A SEA GIRL	60
HOW THE DOG GOT THE WOLF WEAR BOOTS	64
GUSTEK'S MISFORTUNE	67
THE TWO BROTHERS	71
MIRACLE AT THE MILL	75

LARK AND THE WOLF	78
THE TALE OF THE SPELLBOUND PIKE	80
OSTRUDA STONE	82
LAZY GIRL	87
THE DWARF AND THE BEAR	91
NOBLEMAN AND MICHAL	96
PUNISHED FOR GUILE	100
MISFORTUNE	105
THE RAM BROTHER AND THE DUCK SISTER	107
THE SHEPHERD	111
ABOUT TWO GIRLS, A KIND ONE AND A WICKED ONE	114
THE GIRL AND THE PRINCE IN THE COW'S SKIN	117
GOLDEN FISH	122
GOLD TROT	124
HEALING WATER	130
PRINCE AND HIS HELPERS	134
ABOUT THE COCKEREL	139
THE FISHERMAN'S SON AND THE WATER MAN'S DAUGHTER	141
BOY AND HIS DOG AND CAT, AND THE LION CUB	144
THE MAN WHO WENT TO ASK THE SUN	148
THE MAGIC GUN, THE FIDDLE, AND THE BOOTS	151
THE GLASS HILL	155
FEAR	160
TITELITURY	165
THE TAILOR'S WIFE AND THE COUNTESS	168
HOW THE SLUG DEFEATED THE FOX	172

NOTES

We greatly appreciate when our readers take time to submit good reviews for our books.*

*www.amazon.com/dp/1517127998
www.amazon.co.uk/dp/1517127998

Your attention is really appreciated.

Please feel free to share the link* to this book on social networking sites (Facebook, Twitter, etc) or with your friends and colleagues.

*www.createspace.com/5709475
www.amazon.com/dp/1517127998

Other books from this series can be found at the following locations:

With Fire and Sword: A Tale of the Past
Authored by Henryk Sienkiewicz, Translated by S. A. Binion
www.amazon.com/dp/1530493870

With Fire and Sword. An Historical Novel of Poland and Russia
Authored by Henryk Sienkiewicz, Translated by Jeremiah Curtin
www.amazon.com/dp/1530494001

What I Believe
Authored by Leo Tolstoy, Translated by Constantine Popoff
www.amazon.com/dp/1522841199

The Comédienne, For the Love of Children
Authored by Wladyslaw S. Reymont
www.amazon.com/dp/ 1530484367

The Awakening (The Resurrection)
Authored by Leo Tolstoy, Translated by William E. Smith
www.amazon.com/dp/1530465419

Stories Told by Stewardesses
Authored by Sergio Novikov
www.amazon.com/dp/1530142628

Quo Vadis: A Narrative of the Time of Nero
Authored by Henryk Sienkiewicz, Translated by Jeremiah Curtin
www.amazon.com/dp/1530492815

Quo Vadis: A Tale of the Time of Nero
Authored by Henryk Sienkiewicz,
Translated by S. A. Binion, S. Malevsky
www.amazon.com/dp/ 1530492173

In Desert and Wilderness, The Story of a Lighthouse Keeper
Authored by Henryk Sienkiewicz
www.amazon.com/dp/1530494303

In Desert and Wilderness
Authored by Henryk Sienkiewicz
www.amazon.com/dp/1530248019

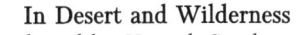

ABOUT THIS BOOK

This book comprises of 50 Polish folk fairy tales.

In order to collect the fairy tales in this book for you, we had been interviewing Polish natives from 1992 to 2012.

These tales are radiant with the Polish people's vitality, filial love for one's parents, and the energy of kindness.

They were collectively created by the Polish nation. Many authors of various origins have adopted these folk motives and tales since then. However, this compilation presents the original folk versions of the tales.

None of these fairy tales has been previously published in this English translation.

They have been lovingly collected and translated into English by publisher Sergiej Nowikow, Polish by spirit and Polish in his deeds, Polish to the core.

P.S.

In order to test our young reader's attention, we have deliberately made seven minor misprints in the book.

Please send a message describing them to
publisher@worker.com
If you are able to spot all of them,
it means you are a true discoverer.

The latest version of the book in a hard copy can be found at the following locations:

in UK & other European countries:
www.createspace.com/5709475
www.amazon.co.uk/dp/1517127998

in the United States & Canada:
www.createspace.com/5709475
www.amazon.com/dp/1517127998

The latest version of the book in electronic form can be found at the following locations:

in Poland:
www.amazon.co.uk/gp/product/B014JMZ8GA

in the United States:
www.amazon.com/gp/product/B014JMZ8GA

in UK:
www.amazon.co.uk/gp/product/B014JMZ8GA

in Canada:
www.amazon.ca/gp/product/B014JMZ8GA

in France:
www.amazon.fr/gp/product/B014JMZ8GA

in Spain:
www.amazon.es/gp/product/B014JMZ8GA

in Japan:
www.amazon.co.jp/gp/product/B014JMZ8GA

in Brazil:
www.amazon.com.br/gp/product/B014JMZ8GA

in Mexico:
www.amazon.com.mx/gp/product/B014JMZ8GA

in Australia:
www.amazon.com.au/gp/product/B014JMZ8GA

in Germany:
www.amazon.de/gp/product/B014JMZ8GA

in India:
www.amazon.in/gp/product/B014JMZ8GA

Made in the USA
Middletown, DE
22 December 2017